BRAVE NEW GIRL

BRAVE NEW GIRL
BRAVE NEW GIRL
BRAVE NEW GIRL

BRAVE NEW GIRL

RACHEL VINCENT

DELACORTE PRESS

Text copyright © 2017 by Rachel Vincent
Jacket art copyright © 2017 by Gustavo Marx/MergeLeft Reps

All rights reserved. Published in the United States by Delacorte Press, an imprint of Random House Children's Books, a division of Penguin Random House LLC, New York.

Delacorte Press is a registered trademark and the colophon is a trademark of Penguin Random House LLC.

randomhouseteens.com

Educators and librarians, for a variety of teaching tools, visit us at RHTeachersLibrarians.com

Library of Congress Cataloging-in-Publication Data
Names: Vincent, Rachel, author.
Title: Brave new girl / Rachel Vincent.
Description: First edition. | New York : Delacorte Press, [2017]. |
Summary: In a world where everyone is the same, Trigger 17 convinces Dahlia 16 that she is unique but this proves that both are flawed, which could lead to dire consequences for their entire genomes.
Identifiers: LCCN 2016027584 | ISBN 978-0-399-55245-8 (hardback) |
ISBN 978-0-399-55247-2 (ebook)
Subjects: | CYAC: Individuality—Fiction. | Conformity—Fiction. | Genetic engineering—Fiction. | Love—Fiction. | Science fiction.
Classification: LCC PZ7.V7448 Br 2017 | DDC [Fic]—dc23

The text of this book is set in 11.5-point Electra.
Interior design by Trish Parcell

Printed in the United States of America
10 9 8 7 6 5 4 3 2 1
First Edition

To the girl I used to be (and the millions out there like her),
who wanted so desperately to be different,
yet feel like she belonged

WHEN I WAS LITTLE, I thought every girl in the world looked just like me, because that's how it is in the nurseries. The only female faces I saw that weren't identical to mine belonged to our nannies, who all looked just like one another, and I believed that when I grew up my face would match theirs.

The day I was promoted from Dahlia 3 to Dahlia 4, my class went to live in the primary dormitory and got to eat in the cafeteria with other kids for the first time. My mind was *blown*. We couldn't read yet, but we all recognized the names printed on the other kids' uniforms because we'd been staring at them on our own clothes all our lives.

The names are all the same, of course. It's the numbers that matter. The numbers and the faces. That first day in the primary cafeteria, most of us were too stunned to eat much.

Poppy 4, my best friend, kept talking about the other faces. The year-five girls all had pale curls and a bunch of little spots on their faces, which our nanny called freckles. The year sixes had brown skin and long, straight black hair.

Poppy wanted freckles *so* badly.

And the boys. We'd seen the year-four boys in the nursery, of course, but the fives and sixes looked as different from the boys we knew as their female counterparts looked from us. That was before we understood about the preservation and equal distribution of genetic traits. All we knew was that in a cafeteria full of four-, five-, and six-year-olds, we were seeing six completely different faces.

Our worldview had just exploded.

But while Poppy stared at face after face full of freckles and Violet reached out to touch each head of smooth, straight hair that passed our table, I studied every uniform I could see, searching for a series of letters that matched my own. Somewhere in that crowd of hundreds of primary-school-aged kids there was a girl named Dahlia 5. She wouldn't look like me, of course. She would look like all the other year fives. But even as a four-year-old, I understood that Dahlia 5 and I were alike on a much more fundamental level.

Hours earlier, she'd been Dahlia 4. She'd been me. And in another year, I would be her. I thought that if I could find her, I would be looking into my own future.

I've never been more wrong about anything in my life.

ONE

My tomatoes smell so good. They are red and ripe and firm, and I would love to pull one from its vine and bite into it like an apple. But I won't, because hydroponic gardeners grow vegetables for the city, not for themselves.

"Why do you always do that?" Sorrel 16 stares at my left hand where it's folded over the edge of the flood table, my fingers dangling in the water. There's a pH tester on the table—it looks like a fat pen—but I rarely use it.

"Dahlia thinks she can tell the pH balance of the water just by touching it," Poppy 16 answers for me, leaning around her own vines to whisper as our instructor wanders closer.

"I'm right, aren't I?" Though my skill doesn't actually come from touching the water; it comes from watching the plants closely. I'm not supposed to take personal pride in the fact that my tomatoes are the brightest, firmest fruit in our class, but I can't figure out how not to. The best I can do is try to hide my pleasure from our instructor. And from the cameras.

My favorite of the tomatoes we've grown so far are the fat red beefsteaks, just begging to be sliced and layered onto a soy burger or a turkey BLT. But I also have a soft spot for the Italian plum variety and the vibrant yellow pear tomatoes, which are about the size of my thumb but bulbous on one end.

Sometimes I wish I could tell the cooks that tomatoes are *not* all alike. But my job is not to design recipes or cook food. My job is to grow vegetables. At least, it will be when my class graduates and joins the trade labor division. As members of the hydroponic gardening union, we will grow vegetables for the city of Lakeview. That's been our fate since before our genome was commissioned by Management.

"Okay, genius." Violet peeks at me from between her vines. Her station is diagonally across from mine, next to Poppy's and opposite Sorrel's in our workstation cube. "What am I doing wrong, then?" she whispers.

Her leaves are curling up at the tips, and her stems have a faint reddish cast. "Magnesium deficiency. Your pH is too low."

"That's not possible," Violet whispers. "I checked the pH yesterday."

"Check again." I hand her the pH tester and she dips it into the water in her flood tray. Her eyes narrow and her jaw clenches. I recognize her frustration because I see that very expression in the mirror every single day. Not that I need a mirror to know what I look like. All I have to do is look around the room.

All twenty students in the year-sixteen girls' hydroponic gardening class have the same brown hair, brown eyes, and fair skin. We are all right-handed. We all have prominent, unattached earlobes and second toes that are longer than the first, and we can all roll our tongues. If I were to step into any of the other trade labor classrooms—electrical, plumbing, cooking, sewing, carpentry, mechanics, landscape gardening, and many, many others—I would see twenty more identical faces and bodies, differentiated from mine only by the bar codes on their wrists and the names on their uniforms. Names like Anise and Julienne. Cornice and Fascia. Gusset and Muslin.

All the girls in the year-sixteen trade labor division were cloned from a single genome designed by a genetic engineer to be healthy, hardy, and smart. And we are.

But some of us are also lazy. Like Violet.

"Dahlia 16!" our instructor, Sorrel 32, calls from across the room.

I freeze as her standard-issue instructor shoes clack closer. Her hand lands on my shoulder and I hold my breath. We're not supposed to talk to our friends during class.

"These Italian plums are gorgeous! When did you start them?" Sorrel 32 lifts the tag dangling from one of my vines and her eyes widen. "Is this an error?" She taps the date on my tag. "These vines can't be only six weeks old."

"They are. I started them on the same day as everyone else." And she must know that. She's been in class every day, including the day we started this tomato unit.

"None of the others are ready to harvest." Her gaze roams the hydroponic greenhouse, skimming tomatoes in various stages of growth. Mine are the most mature. "This is very good work, Dahlia 16."

"I work for the glory of the city," I tell her. But inside I am buzzing with toxic pride. Tomatoes are my favorite, and evidently they like me as much as I like them.

When the instructor releases us from our work-study period, I clean up my station and store my supplies; then I duck into the seedling room to check on my carrots and beets. My six-foot row of plants is only a miniature version of what I'll be responsible for once I graduate, but again, my plants stand out, even in the early stages. Olive 16's beets look strong too, though.

Envy is a child's emotion. Our city's fortitude depends upon the strength of all its members working together—even those of us who just grow vegetables—and Lakeview will be better off if both Olive and I are good at our jobs.

Yet I want to be the better gardener.

6

I try to shake that thought, but I can't dislodge it. I want to be better at tubers than Olive is, just like I wanted to be better than all the others at grains, vines, and legumes. And not just for the glory of Lakeview.

Whether it's shameful or not, I feel a sense of satisfaction when my produce is obviously the best in the class, but not because I've provided the city with the best vegetables I can grow. I'm pleased because the best vegetables I can grow are better than the best vegetables anyone else can grow. It's a strangely self-indulgent gratification.

Being the best *feels good*.

On the tail of that treacherous thought, I realize I've been looking at Olive's plants for too long. Whoever is monitoring the camera feed might have seen my envy and realized that it is driven by personal pride.

Quickly, I check the pH balance of the solution in my carrot flood tray; then I return everything to order and head back into the classroom.

Poppy is waiting for me by the door so we can walk to the cafeteria together. Instead of the green gardening apron with POPPY 16 embroidered at the center, she's now wearing the green classroom jacket with POPPY 16 embroidered over her heart, because after lunch we have a four-hour block of academics. She's holding my jacket as well, but before I can take it from her, Sorrel 32 steps into my path.

Our instructor smiles at me. "Dahlia 16, Management would like to see you."

My throat tries to close around my next breath.

"I'm sure you have no reason to worry," she says. "They've probably just noticed those beautiful Italian plums!"

Sorrel 32 is very nice, but she doesn't know that I studied Olive 16's beets too long. Or that jealousy might have been clear in my expression when I looked at them.

"Now?" My voice sounds breathy and insubstantial.

She nods. "You'll be given a late pass, so you'll have time to finish your lunch with the next class."

I see faces that are different from mine all the time, but I've never sat at a table surrounded by people who don't look just like me. I will stand out.

Nerves trace the length of my spine, but there's no question that I will obey the summons.

I take my jacket from Poppy and she looks almost as anxious about walking to the cafeteria by herself as I am about crossing the common lawn on my own. Students are encouraged to stay in the company of our identicals to maintain our sense of identity and reinforce our purpose and position in the city's structure.

Lakeview is comprised of five bureaus, each with distinct responsibilities. I am a student member of the Workforce Bureau, which is further divided into the trade labor and manual labor divisions. The Arts Bureau provides Lakeview with music and art, including the murals gracing the walls of all the academies and the sculptures dotting the common lawn at neat, measured intervals. The Specialist Bureau gives us medical personnel, scientists, and engineers. The Defense

Bureau trains soldiers for the protection and fortification of the city, and the Management Bureau ensures that everything runs at peak efficiency, with as little waste as possible.

I eat, bunk, work, and learn with the other trade labor division year-sixteen girls. And we're really very fortunate that there are so many of us. I feel sorry for some of the smaller units because so few of the faces they see on a daily basis match their own. It must be hard for them to know where they belong.

Though the clink of utensils and the buzz of conversation call to me from the cafeteria down the hall, I head for the bank of elevators. As I step inside the first to open, I realize that I've never been in an elevator alone. I'm the only one leaving the academy in the middle of the day, and when I cross the first-floor lobby I feel strangely conspicuous and exposed.

Outside, a class of landscape gardeners is busy pulling last month's flowers from the amorphous flower bed winding around the side of the academy, under the supervision of their instructor. The gardeners are light-skinned boys with freckles and brown eyes, crowned by short, dark brown waves. The familiar names—Aspen, Linden, Oleander, Ash—stitched onto all their uniforms end in the number 13.

Beyond the flower beds, another instructor leads a class of little girls with dark skin and poufy curls down a curving sidewalk toward a playground at one end of the common lawn. Movement to my right catches my attention, and I turn to find four large black-clad soldiers from Defense patrolling the common lawn in synchronized steps. Beyond them, a shiny black car rolls down the street, following a special thick, metallic-looking strip of paint called a cruise strip, which guides all the city's vehicles. In the front seat, two men in suits—obviously Management—read from their tablets, tapping their way through menus and messages as the car takes them to work.

Everyone has somewhere to be and something to be doing. Including me. So I swallow my fear and head down the curving path toward the gate leading out of the training ward.

I've spent my entire life in the training ward, splitting my time between the Workforce Academy and my dormitory—first the nursery, then the primary, and now the secondary dorm. And though I'm less than two years from graduating, I've never even seen the residential ward, where my identicals and I will live as adult members of the Workforce Bureau. In fact, I've only been outside of the training ward twice.

At the gate, a soldier named Eckhard 24 watches while I hold my arm beneath a scanner. The red light passes over the bar code on my wrist, and an electronic voice reads the directions that appear on the screen. "Dahlia 16. Proceed to the Management Bureau."

"Do you know which building that is?" the soldier asks me.

"Yes."

I've never been to the Management Bureau, but I saw it once. It's the smallest of the bureaus, because Management requires relatively little personnel. There are so few students training to be managers that their academy is only three stories tall.

By contrast, the Workforce Academy is the biggest building in Lakeview. It has to be. While there may only be twenty girls in all of the year-sixteen Management class, there are *five thousand* sixteen-year-old trade labor students who share my face.

Which is why it feels so odd to be leaving the training ward without a crowd of them around me.

The soldier presses a button, and the gate slides open with a heavy scraping sound. "Thank you for your service," I say as I step out of the training ward.

"Your work honors us all," he replies.

The gate slides shut behind me and I relax a little as I pass the Hydroponic Gardening Center, where my identicals and I will work when we graduate. Poppy hopes we'll be assigned to the grains and grasses unit, because it's the most spacious, but I hope we get vines and climbers. Or anything other than tubers, really.

Beyond the HGC are the Medical Center and the Arts Center. Then I come to a neat row of bureau headquarters in what must be the heart of the city.

The Defense Bureau is a featureless concrete building, squat at only two stories high but broad and deep. The Workforce Bureau is a utilitarian structure of steel and windows, and beyond that stands the Management Bureau, a narrow tower of mirrored glass reflecting sunshine back at the rest of the world as if it's the actual source of the life-giving light.

I jog up the steps and into Management headquarters, then hold my wrist beneath one of the scanners in the lobby. The red light moves over my bar code, and that same electronic voice reads the onscreen instructions.

"Dahlia 16. Proceed to Suite 4C, room 27. Gardening manager Cady 34 is expecting you."

I step into the nearest elevator, where my image stares back at me from the mirrored doors, and for a second the reflection feels like company. When the doors open on the fourth floor, I step into a white-tiled lobby, where a sign directs me to the left, for Suite C, home of Management's gardening unit.

I knock on the door labeled 27 and a woman's voice calls for me to come in.

Cady 34—and everyone else from her division, obviously—is a petite woman with light brown skin and dark eyes.

"Have a seat, Dahlia 16." She gestures to the pair of chairs in front of her desk.

I sit in the one on the right, my palms slick with nervous sweat.

"Your instructor tells me that your produce is consistently among the best, not just in your class but in your entire union."

I blink at her, surprised. Sorrel 32 is obviously pleased with my work, but standing out too much—even for a good reason—is never advisable. Anything that breaks from the norm threatens the efficiency of the system as a whole.

"Sorrel 32 has nominated you for consideration as a future instructor. She believes that your skills could better benefit the city by teaching others to grow food at a higher quality than by growing food yourself. Do you agree?"

I can't remember another adult ever asking my opinion. This is a test. It must be.

My heart races. I don't know the right answer.

"It's not a trick question, Dahlia 16." But Cady 34 isn't smiling, nor does she make any attempt to set me at ease. "Do you believe you could best serve Lakeview as an instructor? Do you want to become an instructor?"

Do I *want* . . . ?

What a strange question.

Selecting me as an instructor is the only way the city of Lakeview will ever acknowledge my hard work and superior skill. But rather than growing tomatoes, carrots, or strawberries in the company of my peers, I'll spend the rest of my life growing other gardeners. Alone.

Is that what I want?

Cady 34 notices my indecision. "You don't need to answer right now. But you should know that you're not the only one being evaluated for this position."

Surprise gets the better of me and I sit straighter in my chair. "Who else are you watching?" It's Olive 16. I know it is.

Cady 34 frowns, and I realize I'm not supposed to care about who else they're considering. This is not a competition. What matters is that Management chooses the person whose instruction of future gardeners will most benefit the city of Lakeview—whether or not I am that person.

"Dahlia, as long as your efforts continue to glorify the city,

13

you have a good chance of being selected as an instructor. But the city of Lakeview has no use for ego or personal pride, and Management won't reward either of those by putting you in a position of authority and instruction over young minds. You are just one pixel out of the thousands required to form a clear image, so you need to focus on that image as a whole. If your arrogance were to be deemed a genetic flaw, Management would have no choice but to recall all"—she glances at something on her tablet screen—"five thousand specimens of your genome. Do you understand what that means?"

Fear weighs me down like shoes made of lead. I nod. Recalling my genome would mean purging every girl in my division.

Five thousand corpses, all wearing my face.

I am numb as I step into the elevator. The doors slide closed and I begin to ascend, because I am so lost in this new fear that I forgot to press a button.

The floor number climbs as I jab at the button marked "L," for lobby, but it doesn't light up, nor does the elevator descend. Someone else has called the elevator.

My rise stops on the tenth floor, and when the doors slide open a cadet from the Defense Bureau steps inside. The name embroidered in white on his black jacket reads TRIGGER 17. He is just months away from starting his life as a full-fledged soldier.

"Thank you for your service," I say as the doors slide shut, because that's all a trade laborer is allowed to say to a cadet or a soldier.

"Your work honors us all," he replies. Then he pushes the "L" button.

The elevator begins to descend, and I sneak a glance up at him because I've never seen his genetic model up close. The geneticist who engineered his genome has certainly brought glory to the city with this design.

Trigger 17 is tall, with skin a few shades deeper than mine and eyes like the night sky—dark and bright. His features have a pleasing strength and symmetry. I've just noticed the way the cadet's hair curls around the top of his left ear when the elevator grinds to a startling halt, throwing me off balance.

As I stumble into the wall, the lights go out. I am trapped in a broken elevator with Trigger 17.

TWO

A panicked sound escapes from my throat. I blink, but the darkness doesn't clear. My hands find the wall, searching for something to grip, but this elevator has no handrail. If it plummets, I will have no way to brace for impact.

Air rushes in and out of my lungs as I slide down the wall to sit on the floor. I can't see anything, so I clutch my knees to my chest and try to stay calm. Someone will come for us. Someone will fix the elevator and turn the light back on. It's just a little malfunction.

The elevator drops several feet. I scream as I am lifted, then slammed down hard enough to bruise my tailbone. My teeth snap together, cutting off my cry, and across the elevator there is a heavier thud of impact, followed by a startled grunt from the cadet.

I can't breathe. Have we run out of air already, or is there something wrong with my lungs?

What if the elevator drops again? What if it falls all the way to the lobby? A gardener's academic block doesn't include much physics or human anatomy; I have no idea what to expect from a plummet to the ground.

I try to suck in a deep breath, but only a weak wheeze escapes my throat. I'm panicking, obviously, and that realization leads to a terrifying certainty: Management won't want an instructor who's prone to panic during emergencies. How could they trust me to calm and lead a class full of children during a crisis if I can't even compose myself?

My throat is closing, and I don't know how to open it. I've forgotten how to—

"Breathe." The cadet's voice echoes in the silent elevator.

Shocked, I can only stare into the dark in his direction. His advice adds a new layer of anxiety to my fear of this confined, unlit space. We're not allowed to converse with members of another bureau beyond the prescribed greetings and any communication required to perform a necessary joint task.

Trigger 17 is violating the fraternization directive.

He must be defective.

The thought sends a chill across my skin. Suddenly the elevator feels even smaller and darker than before. Tighter somehow, as if there isn't enough room for my lungs to expand.

"You have to calm down, or you'll hyperventilate. Is that

what they teach at the Workforce Academy?" the cadet demands softly. "How to panic until you pass out?"

Of course not!

Indignation pierces my fear, but I don't know how to respond without breaking a rule myself. Nor can I understand why I want so badly to do that very thing. Is that impulse a sign of a defect in my own genome?

"You don't have to say anything. I know Workforce isn't taught to take risks," he says. But he can't possibly know that for sure, any more than I know what Defense cadets are taught. Even if he is right.

I want him to stop talking. When Management finds out that he violated the fraternization directive, they might assume I did too. Because why would he keep talking if he got no response?

Would telling him to stop be a violation, or might Management consider that a necessary communication? I don't know, and the possibility that I might be found guilty by association makes me feel as if not just the elevator but the entire world is closing in on me.

I'm breathing too fast again.

"Okay. Just calm down and listen." Clothing rustles as he shifts on the other side of the elevator. "Concentrate on the sound of my voice and you'll be fine."

His voice.

I wish I wasn't hearing it yet. . . . It's much lower and smoother than the voices of the boys in my bureau. I find it oddly pleasant.

"Back when I was Trigger 7, a boy named Mace 7 locked me in a closet during a tour of the Defense Bureau. The space was dark, and it smelled weird, and there must have been an air-conditioning unit nearby, because all I could hear was the growling of the motor and the whistle of air through some massive vent. I tried to yell for help, but no one could hear me over all that noise. At first I just wanted to curl up in the corner. But that would be behavior unbefitting a future soldier."

I can picture it—a young Defense cadet alone in the dark, determined to stay true to his training in spite of his fear—and I want to hear more. Maybe because I've never been spoken to by a cadet. Maybe because I've never truly considered what life is like for members of another bureau. But probably because Trigger 17's voice is captivating. It commands attention.

He should stop talking for his own good, but I hope he won't.

"I was in there for hours," Trigger continues in the dark, and since I can't see him, it's almost as if this moment isn't really happening. As if I'm imagining it. "I tried to find a creative solution to an impossible situation, as I'd been trained. I opened all the boxes, but they only held paper. I stacked them to try to reach a vent in the wall, but it was too high. I tried to pull the pins from the door hinges but couldn't without any tools."

I listen, fascinated, and it's like I'm there with Trigger 7 in that storage closet, trying to rescue myself through methods no Dahlia 7 would ever have thought of. Methods no Dahlia, Poppy, or Violet would ever have been taught.

"No one noticed I was missing until they wound up with an extra tray at dinner, and even then it took them so long to find me that I thought when they finally opened the door, they'd be greeted by my emaciated corpse."

My chest feels tight at the thought that we could be trapped in this elevator for hours. That our absences could go unnoticed.

"My point is that someone *did* come, eventually, and when my instructor finally opened that door, he found neither an emaciated corpse nor a crying child. He found a cadet standing at attention, reciting everything he'd learned in class that week between sets of jumping jacks.

"They're going to find us much more quickly than they found me that day, because it won't take long for someone to notice that the elevator doesn't work. And when they open the doors, what they're going to find is Dahlia 16, composed and confidently reciting a list of evergreen trees suitable to grow in warm climates. Or whatever they teach you gardeners."

He noticed my name. I'm surprised by the warmth in my cheeks. Then I laugh out loud when I realize what he's said.

"Hydroponic gardeners don't grow—" I slap both hands over my mouth, and my face burns even hotter with guilt for my infraction.

"The power's out, so the cameras don't work," he says. "And I won't tell."

But that isn't the point. The only way society can function efficiently is through the division of duties and personnel into

20

distinct and independent spheres. We learn that before we're even old enough to walk. No good can come of my speaking to Trigger 17.

Yet somehow I'm breathing normally, finally. His story distracted me from the dark elevator and the possibility of plummeting to our deaths.

The light comes back on and I exhale. Then I realize that the elevator looks too dim. Too yellow.

"Automatic emergency lights." Trigger points at the corner over my head, and I twist to look. "The camera is still off."

There's no red power light.

My focus falls from the camera and lands on his face, but I don't realize I'm staring until his gaze meets mine. His lips turn up into a small smile and his left brow rises.

I look away, my face burning again, and Trigger laughs. "There's no rule against looking." At the edge of my vision, I see him shrug. "I'm going to look."

My face is on fire now, but I can't stop him from staring at me. I can't even tell him to stop without breaking a rule. So I steel my nerves and stare back at him.

He has thick dark eyebrows and long lashes. A straight nose. A square jaw and generous lips. And that's where my gaze snags. I can't look away from his mouth, and I have no idea why.

"You're beautiful, Dahlia."

I frown and my focus finds his eyes again. "Beautiful" isn't a concept we apply to people. There is beauty in the graceful arch of a delicate growing vine or the plump perfection of grapes ready to be picked. There is beauty in the rambling shoreline of the lake that gives our city its name and in the explosion of color across the sky when the sun goes down.

Nature is full of beauty, but we are not made by nature. We are made by geneticists—scientists from the Specialist Bureau who know how to assemble human DNA like a construction worker assembles buildings, carefully piecing together the necessary components until the result has both the desired form and function.

Form.

Now I understand. I'm not sure the word *beauty* can be applied to my genome, but suddenly the term seems custom-made to describe his.

But he can't take credit for his features, and they don't belong to him alone, so what would be the point of such a compliment? The flush in my cheeks crawls down my neck at just the idea of voicing my thoughts. There could be no more pointless a violation of the fraternization directive than to waste forbidden words telling Trigger how pleasing I find the structure of his face.

Yet he's just told me that very thing.

He glances again at the name embroidered on my jacket. "A dahlia is a flower, right?"

Actually, dahlia is a genus of tuberous plant consisting of many different species. It is a very diverse genus, which displays a wide range of sizes, colors, and types. And yes, many produce blooms. He's walked by several hundred of them every day for the past month since one of the landscape gardening classes installed them in the flower bed on the east side of the secondary dormitory.

But I can't tell him any of that, so I only nod. That's not really fraternizing, right?

"Do you know what a trigger is?" he asks, and I shake my head.

"It's the movable piece by which a mechanism is operated. In most contexts, the word refers to the part of a gun you pull with your finger to fire a bullet. And in that other context"—he smiles and shrugs—"it refers to me. I'm Trigger."

I am transfixed. His name comes from the part of a weapon used to kill people. Which is appropriate for a cadet, who is himself a weapon presumably used to do that very thing. I can hardly imagine how different his classes must be from mine. I learn how to nurture life, and he learns how to take it.

None of my identicals would ever have locked me in a closet. Not even Calla, who's more like a thorn than a flower. Are things so different in the Defense Bureau?

"You said you're a hydroponic gardener?" Trigger says, and I frown at the reminder that I've actually spoken to him. "So what's your favorite thing to grow? Fruit? Vegetable?"

I hesitate, because technically the terms *fruit* and *vegetable* are not in opposition. A fruit is the edible part of a plant that bears seeds, and a vegetable is any part of any edible plant—including fruit—that can be served as part of a savory meal.

23

But no cadet would have any reason to know that.

Trigger laughs over my hesitation. "Something that fits into both categories? Must be the tomato."

He looks smug. He clearly has no idea how lucky his guess is, because many foods fit into both categories. But he's right.

"I like tomatoes too," he says. "And nuts. My favorites are pecans and walnuts."

I laugh, because neither of those are true nuts. They're seeds.

"What's so funny?" he demands, and I *really* want to tell him. But if Management wanted him to know the difference between nuts and seeds and kernels, they would have cloned him from a different genome. All Trigger 17 needs to know about his food is how good it tastes and how much energy it provides.

His eyes narrow. "Okay, so you may be the plant expert, but have you ever eaten a nut right off the ground? Or a peach plucked from the tree? Because that's what we do when we go out on patrol or war games."

Envy burns deep in my chest. I've been growing plants my entire life but have *never* been allowed to sample one before the cooks-in-training chop them up, boil them down, and serve them all mushy and nearly tasteless on my cafeteria tray.

We learned in class that soldiers have to be able to cook for themselves on long missions. "Are you training to be a field cook?" I don't realize I've actually spoken the question aloud until Trigger 17's brows rise.

Trigger laughs. "No. I'm infantry division, Special Forces union."

Yet he gets to pluck fruit straight from the tree. Suddenly my envy flares into an explosion of anger. He has no idea what it takes to grow a vegetable from a single seed. To keep the pH balance of the water steady. To trim, replant, and nurture. Why should he get to taste food right from its source when I cannot?

"Dahlia? I'm sorry. I didn't mean to—"

"What does a tomato taste like? Fresh from the vine?"

He shrugs. "I've never come across tomatoes growing wild, but I've had spinach so fresh you have to wash the dirt from it in a stream. I've had wild onions. And carrots. And yams. And several gourds."

I am a *storm* of envy now, ready to rain spite all over him. How can a soldier trained to do nothing more complicated with food than eat it be so much more experienced with it than I am?

I know Management has reasons for the way it runs the city, and I'm not supposed to understand those reasons. But I can't see how this could *possibly* make sense.

It's gotten warm in the elevator, and Trigger unbuttons the cuffs of his jacket so he can roll the sleeves up. My gaze stops on his newly exposed flesh and my eyes widen.

"You look like you want to ask me something," he says, and I can tell by the way he's displaying his right arm that he knows exactly what I want to say.

But I'm starting to understand why fraternization is against the rules. I cannot afford to indulge in uninhibited speech, even here, where there's no one else to hear it. What if I can't stop talking to him once I begin?

"You've already spoken to me," he says. "Stopping now is pointless."

He's right. And I can't resist. "What happened to your arm?" I ask, studying the long, jagged scar winding around the flesh below his elbow.

Trigger remains focused on my face. "I got snagged trying to avoid a knife. It looks nasty, but there's no permanent nerve or muscle damage."

I only vaguely know what that means. What I do understand is that no two scars are alike. If Trigger 17 were to take off the jacket bearing his name, I would still be able to identify him at a glance.

"So you stand out." Gardeners don't have distinctive scars unless something goes horrifically wrong, which hasn't happened in my lifetime, and the thought of being so conspicuous sets me on edge. "You're different from your identicals." Does that mean he's no longer an identical?

If so, what is he?

The Administrator has no identicals, because when she ascended to her position as the head of Management, her genome was retired—a rare and extraordinary honor. But everyone else is one of many. A part of the whole. That's the way it's supposed to be.

Trigger shrugs. "Most cadets have scars by the time they

get promoted to year thirteen," he says. "So we're all alike, in that we're each a little different."

My eyes close as I try to puzzle through that. Soldiers are *all* different from their identicals. They fit in *because* they're different.

That's so absurd it almost makes sense.

"Any other questions?" Trigger says, drawing my thoughts back from where they've wandered. "We may be stuck here awhile."

"What happened to Mace 7?" I ask. "How was he punished?"

"Um . . . I think he had to mop our entire dormitory floor for a month. Or maybe he scrubbed toilets. Those are the most common punishments at our academy."

There are *common* punishments at the Defense Academy? I can count on one hand the number of times a girl from my division has required punishment.

For a moment, I can only stare at Trigger. "Why—"

But then the lights come back on, blinding us with the sudden glare. I stand as the elevator lurches into motion again and begins to descend smoothly toward the lobby level. One glance at the camera overhead confirms that it's functioning. I can't ask Trigger 17 my last question, and I will probably never know the answer.

I don't even dare look him in the eye.

When the doors slide open, we are greeted by a small crowd of Management members in dark suits and skirts and mechanics in gray coveralls. Cady 34 looks relieved to see me in one piece, but the quick flick of her gaze toward Trigger 17 is telling. She knows we were trapped in the dark together for nearly an hour, with nothing but fear to feed growling bellies and wandering minds. But there's no evidence that we broke any rules.

"Your work honors us all," Trigger says, gesturing for me to precede him into the lobby, and his voice is the epitome of professional detachment. There is no sign of the boy who risked punishment to distract me from terror and panic.

I give him a formal nod and try to follow his lead, even though my guts are twisting with fear and my lungs feel ready to burst with a strange, exhilarating excitement.

We have a secret.

In my entire life, I've never had a secret more important than having seen Iris 5 take an extra cookie from the snack tray back in the primary dorm.

Even if I never see Trigger 17 again, he and I have this secret to share. I am on fire with the knowledge that we broke one of the most consequential rules and no one else has any idea. Or at least no one can prove what they might suspect.

I don't know what to do with that knowledge, other than swallow it and let it warm me from the inside. So that's what I do.

"Thank you for your service." I step into the lobby, and Cady 34 guides me away from the elevator, giving me instructions for how to get a late lunch and make up the class time I've missed. As she ushers me toward the front door of the Management Bureau, I glance back to find Trigger standing alone. He is a cadet, and cadets must be independent and creative. He will procure his own missed lunch.

Maybe he'll pluck peaches and dig up carrots growing in the wild.

His gaze meets mine and he smiles—just the tiniest up-turn of lips I no longer hesitate to label beautiful. Then he turns and walks off in the opposite direction, and I know that though I may see his face all over the city for the rest of my life, I will likely never see Trigger 17 again.

THREE

I wake up with a strange ache in my chest and Trigger 17's face lingering behind my eyelids, and though I've woken in the same bed since the day I was promoted to Dahlia 11, for a moment I have no idea where I am. Then Poppy comes into focus, leaning over me from the side of my bunk. Her hand is on my shoulder. Her frown is trained down at me, and when I see that she's already dressed, I understand.

I've overslept. Again.

"Dahlia, we're going to be late," she repeats, and I practically throw myself out of bed onto the floor. A future instructor would never be late.

"What's going on with you?" Violet demands as I pull a gray dress from the closet we share. All our dresses and shirts and pants are the same, because mass production is efficient

30

and we are all the same size. The only variation is in our jackets and aprons, which have our names embroidered on them. "You've been distracted for days."

For eight days, to be exact. Since the day I got trapped in that elevator.

"I'm just having trouble sleeping."

"You should tell Medical," Sorrel says from the bathroom, wiping a streak of toothpaste from her chin.

But Medical can't know about the source of my dreams or the fear that my secret will be discovered, and the more I think about that, the more reckless my fraternization violation feels.

Yet even my mounting fear after the fact can't diminish the thrill that travels down my spine every time I think about being stuck in the elevator with Trigger 17. Every time I see his identicals marching across the common lawn or jogging in formation. I don't know what this feeling is. I don't understand why my hands suddenly feel so empty. Why I reach out for him in my dreams.

"Nothing's wrong," I insist as I pull my dress over my head. "I just had a bad dream."

"Is it Management?" Poppy smooths back her wavy brown hair and secures it with an elastic band. "Is this about your meeting with Cady 34?"

"Maybe." I drop my nightclothes into the laundry chute built into the wall, where they slide toward the basement to wait for students from the manual labor division to wash, dry, and fold them. "It was unnerving, being called out by myself." Technically that's not a lie. "I'm just . . ."

Violet and Sorrel pause in their morning routines to frown at me as my thought trails into silence.

"She's nervous." Poppy steps into the bathroom and runs water over her toothbrush. "Because she's being considered for an instructor position."

Sorrel's jaw drops open. Violet's brow furrows above narrowed brown eyes.

"I'm sorry. I didn't want to tell you, in case I don't make it."

Violet's frown deepens. "But you told Poppy."

"She tells me everything." Poppy turns on her toothbrush and sticks it into her mouth, leaving me to dig my way out of that hole on my own.

"I don't tell her *everything*. Besides, Violet, you didn't tell me when Calla—"

"Tell us what you haven't told Poppy!" Sorrel whispers, sinking onto her bottom bunk to put on her shoes.

"That's not what I meant. There's nothing to tell." I'm starting to think I'm a terrible liar, and for the first time in my life that prospect bothers me.

Sorrel studies me, and for a second I think she'll press the issue. Then Violet throws a shoe at her. "Come on! I'm not going to be late just because she can't make it out of bed on time!"

Sorrel stands reluctantly.

"Go on," Poppy says. "I'll light a fire under Dahlia and we'll meet you in the cafeteria."

As soon as the door closes behind our identicals, Poppy turns on me. "Is it the boy?" she whispers, too low for the camera mounted in the corner to pick up. "Did you dream about him again?"

I haven't told anyone else about Trigger 17. I *can't* tell anyone else. Sorrel is legitimately concerned about me, but she tells Violet everything, and Violet likes to be liked. She'll tell everyone.

"Yes." I run water over my toothbrush and stare at myself in the mirror. I look the same, but something *feels* different. I can't get him out of my head. "I don't understand it," I tell her as I squeeze toothpaste onto my brush. "I don't know what made me talk to him. And I can't figure out why every time I close my eyes, he's there. Right behind my eyelids. Smiling." There's something about his smile. It gives me a strange, unsteady feeling deep in my stomach.

"It sounds weird." Poppy grabs a pair of socks from my drawer and sticks the folded bundle into my left shoe. "We see boys all the time, and I've never dreamed about one. They're no more interesting than our own identicals. Less so, really."

"I know." But Trigger is different from the boys in the year-sixteen hydroponic gardening class. "Poppy." I turn to her with toothpaste foam in the corners of my mouth. "He's . . . beautiful." I can't figure out how else to explain. "And he's *dangerous*," I whisper, just in case the camera in our bedroom can pick up audio from the bathroom.

Poppy's reflection in the mirror goes still. "Why are you saying that like it's an advantage?"

"I don't know!"

She lowers her voice and frowns at me in the mirror. "He *spoke* to you, Dahlia."

"I'm aware." I run water into the sink to add audio camouflage.

"He put you at risk. He put us *all* at risk."

"I know, and he *terrifies* me. But at the same time, thinking about him makes me feel like I'm at the end of a relay race. Like my whole body is alive and I can't catch my breath."

Poppy's frown deepens. "Dahlia, I think you may be ill. That sounds like some kind of virus."

"I'm not sick," I whisper as I cross into the bedroom to pull on my shoes and socks. But something is definitely wrong. Or at least . . . different.

"Dahlia!" Poppy whispers fiercely as she sinks onto my bunk next to me. "You *spoke* to him!"

There's no use denying it. She knows me too well.

"I couldn't help it. The power was out, so the cameras were off and he was so *fascinating*! He doesn't think about things the same way we do. We were like two people standing in opposite corners of the same room—we see all the same things but from totally different perspectives." I want to know what else he sees. I want to know *how* he sees things. I want to know why his view is so different from mine.

I want to know *everything*.

"Okay, we can't talk about this anymore," Poppy says as I tie my other shoe. "Ever again. This is unsafe, Dahlia."

"I'm sorry to have dragged you into it."

She shrugs. "I'm in it anyway. We all are." Because what one identical does affects all the others. "That's why you can't tell anyone else about this."

"I know." And the truth is that I don't want to. This is *my* secret. It may be the only one I ever have.

Poppy and I greet our identicals in the cafeteria, and as I spear a clump of scrambled eggs with my fork I scan the crowd out of habit, looking for Dahlia 17. I find her easily; she always sits in the same place. Her roommates are the Violet, Sorrel, and Poppy from the year-seventeen class, but she seems to be closer to Iris and Rose. I wish I could hear what they're talking about. They're just months away from joining the workforce at year eighteen, and I'm dying to know what advanced hydroponic techniques I have yet to learn. What glimpses of life as an adult they've already seen.

I'll know all that for myself soon, but patience has never been among my gifts. Poppy says my plants must feel the same way, which is why they mature so quickly. I don't know if that's true, but I can't shake the feeling that, much like the plants they grow, my friends are in no hurry to see or experience anything new. They never seem to think about the future or what it might bring.

I can't figure out why I feel so different, or why meeting Trigger 17 has highlighted all those differences. But I know much better than to ask.

For weeks I see Trigger 17's face everywhere I turn, and I can't decide whether this new frequency is real or imagined. I've probably seen his genome all my life but never had reason to notice. Now every time I see a formation of year-seventeen cadets, my gaze betrays me. I'm losing focus. During sports practice my soccer kicks go wild. I drop the relay baton. I lose count of the seedlings I'm supposed to be inventorying.

Then, on one warm early fall afternoon more than three weeks after we were rescued from the broken elevator, I step out of the secondary dormitory in line between Poppy and Sorrel and am stunned to see Trigger 17 marching in formation with a squad of twelve cadets.

His head turns slightly and he sees me.

My step falters and my chest feels tight. I know it's him without checking for his name. I can see it in the way his gaze lingers. In the subtle upturn of his lips. In the red braid over his shoulder.

How have I never noticed that most cadets don't wear the braid?

Each of his classmates wears a backpack heavy enough to press indentations into his shoulders. Their boots are muddy. Their uniforms are layered with dust and they look tired. They've obviously come from some kind of training mission outside the city.

Poppy follows my gaze before I realize I'm staring. "What's wrong?" she asks.

"Nothing. I . . . Did you know they get to eat vegetables picked right out of the ground?"

"Who?" Sorrel whispers, glancing back at us over her shoulder.

"The Defense cadets. You know how they have to cook their own food when they're out in the wild?" I ask, and my roommates nod. "They don't carry food with them. They eat whatever they can find out there. Growing wild."

"How do you know that?" Sorrel asks.

Poppy gives me a warning look, but I already know I've said too much. I shrug. "I heard it somewhere."

"Better them than us," Sorrel says, but I think she's wrong. I know we grow food more efficiently than it could ever grow from the ground, and I know that our specially engineered strains are hardier and healthier than anything found in the wild. Still, I'd like to see how things used to be. How they still are outside the city.

"Isn't that class a little small for Defense?" Violet whispers from behind Poppy.

"They're Special Forces." But as soon as the words are out, I wish I could stuff them back into my mouth. I'm not supposed to know anything about Defense. So I improvise. "Everything special is produced in limited quantities. Like geneticists."

"I heard geneticists are cloned in batches of ten," Piper adds, and I smile at her, thankful for the change of subject. "And their education is so intense that they don't graduate until year twenty-five."

"*I* heard they're *six* to a class," Violet says. She always argues. "And they don't finish school until they're in year thirty. They're the most elite identicals in the world."

I'm pretty sure that Special Forces cadets are at least as elite as geneticists, but I let her statement stand because no one is focused on Trigger's squad anymore. Except me.

I wonder where they go, outside the city. I wonder what they do. I wonder what the air smells like in the wild. The plants in our gardening lab smell so good they never fail to make me hungry, but I've never smelled them in their natural environment, where the scents are free to mingle with the other aromas of nature.

Before I realize it, we've arrived at the delivery bay behind the Workforce Academy, where carts of gardening supplies are waiting to be unloaded. I try to concentrate on counting and lifting and recording the inventory, but all I can think about is the wild. Unlike a landscape gardener, I've never sunk my fingers into the dirt. I've never pulled a plant from the earth. I've never seen trees growing in any formation other than the meticulously planned, geometrically precise layout of the city's lawns and orchards.

How wild is the wild, exactly?

"Dahlia!" Iris 16 snaps softly, and I look down to realize that liquid fertilizer is dripping onto my shoe from the jug I've just lifted from the delivery cart. "How could you not notice the leak?" she demands. "These bottles are standing a quarter inch deep in liquid fertilizer!"

I glance into the crate and see that Iris is right. I haven't been able to truly concentrate since I met Trigger 17. I want to know what his bureau is taught. I want to see the wild for myself. I want to experience the things Trigger gets to see, touch, and taste.

I want to talk to him again.

The thought that anyone other than Poppy might find out about my ambition and dissatisfaction scares me to death. But I still want dangerous things, even though I know how very dangerous they are.

"Dahlia."

I look up, startled, when Poppy takes the leaking jug from me and sets it back in the crate. "Are you still not sleeping well?" she asks while Iris shakes her head in dismay.

Actually, I look forward to lights-out every night, in case I dream about Trigger 17. Only in my dreams can he and I meet, talk, and look at each other with impunity. But Poppy is trying to help me explain myself.

"I'm fine," I assure them both. "I just got distracted."

Poppy looks even more worried. A future instructor cannot be subject to distraction.

"You're going to have to report that as damaged." Iris nods at the crate where the leaking jug now sits. "And you'll have to change your shoes."

I follow her pointed gaze to see that a puddle of liquid fertilizer has formed around my left sneaker.

"Go on," Poppy says. "I'll take care of the report." Before I can argue, she kneels next to the screen built into the side of the automatic delivery cart and pulls up the inventory chart for the current shipment. She taps on the fertilizer count and reports one damaged jug. Then she slides her wrist beneath the scanner built into the side of the cart and says, "Lakeview central warehouse."

The screen confirms the destination and shows the route it will take; then the cart rolls forward, carrying its damaged goods out of the delivery bay and onto the narrow road that runs behind the row of academies, following the cruise strip.

"Dahlia," Poppy says as she stands, staring at my messy shoe. "Go change."

With a distracted nod, I turn and report the incident to Sorrel 32, who releases me to return to the dormitory and change my shoe. "You may select a classmate to accompany you," she says.

"That's okay. I'll be fine on my own." And anyone I took with me would notice just how distracted I have become.

Sorrel 32 gives me a strange look, and as I head across the common lawn I wonder if I've given the wrong answer. Should a future instructor still be reluctant to leave the company of her identicals? Is learning to work independently from her sisters the most difficult part of instructor training?

Is this supposed to be harder for me than it is?

Alone in my dorm room, I take off my shoes and drop them into the exchange chute, which is used for supplies we don't need replaced every day, like shoes, jackets, and toothbrushes. Only one of my shoes is dirty, but much like me and my identicals, one shoe doesn't travel alone.

Usually.

A second later, a red light flashes to the right of the chute. I pull open the drawer recessed into the wall to find a fresh pair of sneakers waiting for me.

The fertilizer has also dripped onto my top, so I pull it off and drop it into the laundry chute; then I open the dresser drawer labeled with my name and pull out one of my spare shirts. It feels oddly lumpy.

I sit on the bed to unfold my shirt, but I stop, startled, when I see what has been hidden between the layers of cotton.

It's a carrot. But it isn't any of the varieties we grow in the hydroponic lab. This carrot is paler, thinner, and knobbier than any I've ever produced. The stem and blooms have been removed, but the brown smudges in the gray cotton are unmistakable.

This is a wild carrot. Dirt still clings to it.

My pulse jumps, but my excitement is quickly eclipsed by a bolt of fear. I glance up at the camera in the corner of the room and fold the shirt back over the carrot, hoping my arm has blocked it from view. And that no one is currently monitoring the feed from my room.

In the bathroom—the only place where there are no cameras—I unfold my shirt over the sink. Tiny clods of dirt fall into the basin, and I stare at them, fascinated. This dirt is much paler and slightly redder than the soil the landscape gardeners use, because this soil isn't fertilized and tilled, nor does it come delivered in bags from the central warehouse.

This dirt is *earth*. It is wild, free, and fragrant. It reminds me of the time I had to miss a soccer game because of a sprained ankle when I was Dahlia 10. I sat on the sidelines and picked through the grass beneath me, looking for earthworms. My fingernails were caked with the earth, and they smelled like grass, life, and all things green.

That's what this carrot smells like.

Trigger 17.

Only a cadet would have access to vegetables grown in the wild. No one else would have any reason to give one to me. No one else would know how to avoid the cameras well enough to sneak onto my floor of the dormitory, then plant a carrot in my drawer.

My thoughts racing, I turn on the faucet and rinse the carrot. It's long and thin, with a cordlike fibrous length trailing from the tip. I dry the vegetable on a hand towel and lift it for a taste. My mouth waters. But I can't bite into it.

If I eat the carrot, it will be gone; but I want to keep it. I *need* to keep this secret, for proof that I'm not dreaming the whole thing. I want to be able to touch this wild vegetable when no one is looking and know that Trigger risked everything to give it to me.

This contraband carrot is evidence that he's still thinking about me, just like I'm still thinking about him.

I kneel to pick up the shirt where it has fallen on the floor, and sticking out from the material I notice the torn edge of a small piece of wrinkled paper. It looks like some kind of brown wrapping. The narrow, scrawling handwriting on it reads *18th-floor landing. 6:35 p.m.*

My stomach flips. I'm not allowed to use the stairwell except in an emergency. I'm not allowed to talk to students from other bureaus unless we're working on a joint project. And I'm certainly not allowed to lie to my instructors about where I'm going and what I'm doing.

The very idea of breaking all three of those rules to meet with a boy who should not fascinate me like he does is both terrifying and exhilarating. And completely unthinkable.

But six-thirty-five is in the middle of dinner. I could conceivably excuse myself to use the restroom, then sneak onto the landing. There are no cameras in the stairwell.

But if I get caught . . .

I don't even want to imagine what will happen if Trigger 17 and I are discovered. If Management finds out about the deviant thoughts and feelings I now spend every waking moment trying to hide. If they find out about what can only be a massive flaw in my genome. *Both* of our genomes, evidently.

I can't meet Trigger. I *cannot* put my sisters in danger of being recalled.

I shouldn't keep the carrot. It's a dangerous memento. Yet I can't bring myself to part with it. If I eat it—the only safe way to dispose of it—I will lose the tangible certainty that this moment actually happened.

Instead I wrap the note around the carrot and fold them both back into my shirt. Then I rinse all the dirt from the sink and flush the toilet so that anyone listening from the camera feed will think I had a legitimate reason to be in the restroom.

43

In the bedroom, I tuck the shirt-wrapped carrot and note into the back of my drawer and take out a clean top. I hastily pull on both my shirt and shoes, then I head out across the lawn again on my way back to the Workforce Academy.

There is a carrot in my drawer.

It's all I can think about.

FOUR

Voices rise from all around me in the eighteenth-floor cafeteria, and no one seems to mind that the food line is moving extraordinarily slowly. The landscape gardening girls are dragging their feet on purpose. Or am I imagining that?

As I shuffle forward behind Poppy, Sorrel, and Violet, surrounded by our own identicals as well as students from the year-fifteen and year-seventeen classes, my gaze keeps wandering toward the glass wall at the end of the cafeteria. Through it I can see the offices where the eighteenth-floor conservator and her staff of supervisors work when they're not inspecting dorm rooms, scheduling field days, inventorying supplies, sending sick residents to the Medical Center, and generally maintaining a clean and efficient dorm environment.

At the end of that same hall is the stairwell, two doors down from my room. If I were to excuse myself to go to the restroom, I'd only have to walk a few extra feet to go into the stairwell instead. There's a good chance no one would notice.

But what if someone does?

Olive 16 pokes my shoulder, and I turn to see that the line has moved forward without me. Poppy holds her wrist beneath the scanner. There is a whisper of moving parts, then the steel door slides up, revealing her tray.

Her dinner is just like mine. It's just like Olive's, and Violet's, and Sorrel's. We are all the same, and since our physical exertion level is very similar to that of most of the other trade labor unions, our nutritional needs are all virtually identical.

Poppy moves down the line to accept her carton of skim milk and bottle of water while I slide my wrist beneath the scanner in front of the meal dispenser. My tray comes out just like hers did, and as I move forward in line I turn for another glimpse of the stairwell door.

Instead I see a year-seventeen cadet standing in the hallway with a red braid over his shoulder and a tablet under one arm. He's obviously waiting to see my floor's conservator, but he's staring through the cafeteria window at me.

Our gazes lock, and though his expression doesn't change—not even a flicker of a smile—his eyes seem to light up. He's found me almost instantly, even though I am surrounded by my identicals and he's too far away to read the names embroidered on our clothing.

How does he know that I'm me?

"Seriously, Dahlia, I'd like to eat sometime this century,"

Olive says, and I tear my gaze away from Trigger's as if he is a hot coal I've just touched with my bare hand.

I shuffle forward again and accept my bottle of water and carton of milk; then I'm through the line. I dare another glance at him as I make my way to the stainless steel table where my roommates are already seated, but he's gone into the conservator's office. Or maybe he's already in the stairwell waiting for me.

The clock over the door reads 6:25.

I can't meet Trigger. I'd be sealing the fate of five thousand girls—of Poppy and Sorrel and Violet—if I get caught. But I scarf down my dinner anyway, just in case I decide to go, because I'm expected to eat everything on my tray before I leave the cafeteria.

As I chew, I scan the cafeteria for Dahlia 17. She sits several tables away, facing me, and as I watch, she brushes a shoulder-length blond curl back from her freckled face.

Would her genome be so tempted to break the rules? So captivated by a boy with a pleasing aesthetic and a deep voice?

"Dahlia, you look like a horse at a trough." Violet cuts into my thoughts and I look up to see all three of my roommates watching as I shovel one forkful after another into my mouth.

"Sorry," I say around a mouthful of black beans. "I'm starving."

I try to eat more slowly, pretending I'm paying attention as Sorrel complains about the quality of her vines and Iris leans in to give her some truly generic advice. But all I really see is

47

the clock over the door. The digital numbers seem stuck at 6:31. Has time actually stopped?

Finally, the conservator's office door opens and I freeze when Trigger 17 emerges. He glances into the cafeteria briefly, but I can't tell whether he's found me before he turns and marches with a cadet's formal bearing and confidence toward the stairwell.

No one tries to stop him. Are cadets allowed to use the stairs rather than the elevators? Is that part of their physical conditioning?

My leg begins to bounce beneath the table as I watch him walk away. I can't even taste my food anymore. I want to follow him. My body is in the cafeteria, but the rest of me is already in the stairwell, asking him about the carrot, and the wild, and whatever mission or war game took him out of the city. Asking him if he's seen the great, winding channel of water that Riverbend was named for in the mountains that sandwich Valleybrook.

I want to hear his voice, but even more I want to watch his lips as they form the words, and I have no idea why. That seems like an odd thing to crave, yet I do.

Knowing that he's just a hallway away, waiting for me, is more than I can stand. I don't even realize I intend to leave the cafeteria until I'm already on my feet, my empty tray in hand.

"Dahlia?" Poppy stares up at me. "Where are you going?"

"Bathroom." I step back from the stainless steel stool bolted to the floor. "My stomach feels . . . bad."

"Maybe that's because you inhaled your food," Violet says, and I nod because that sounds more plausible than anything I've come up with.

On my way out of the cafeteria, I drop my empty tray into the recycling chute, then tell the supervisor on duty that I'm going to the restroom. She lets me pass, and I can't believe how easy it is. The possibility that I might be sneaking out to break a rule doesn't seem to occur to her, because we are not wired to break the rules. Because, to my knowledge, no one before me has ever tried anything this bold.

Is this what Trigger has figured out? That unless we wave our misbehavior in their faces like a flag, our supervisors and instructors will only see what they expect to see?

My heart pounds as I walk down the hall, and my steps match its rhythm until I'm just feet from my dorm room and only a few more feet from the stairwell. I look over my shoulder at the last minute to make sure I'm not being watched.

No one is looking at me. But I can't help looking at them. Several hundred people are still seated in the cafeteria, and hundreds of them are wearing my face. Spread out over several dozen other floors are thousands more who look just like us. Right now, they are talking and eating, blissfully ignorant of the fact that I'm about to put all of their lives in danger so I can ask a boy I'm not supposed to have met about things I'm not supposed to know.

Suddenly I feel very selfish. I don't have the right to take what I want at the expense of their lives. Just because my genome has flaws—these strange thoughts and urges are

49

evidence of that—doesn't mean that I have to act on them. Right?

Now what I see in the cafeteria is not hundreds of my identicals finishing up their lean chicken breasts, lightly buttered corn, and black beans but a room full of prone corpses staring up at the ceiling with empty eyes. Hundreds of dead bodies that all look just like I do.

My pulse races so fast the hallway begins to blur in front of me.

I glance at the door to the stairwell. I know Trigger is standing right behind it. My hand itches to grab the doorknob. But I slide my wrist beneath the scanner next to my dorm room door instead.

For the next ten minutes, I hold a folded shirt and feel the carrot hidden inside it while I fight the tears pooling in my eyes.

I don't even know why I'm crying.

FIVE

The next two weeks are hell.

I can't stop myself from looking for Trigger every time I see a squad of marching cadets, even when they're not from year seventeen, but now I'm not sure I actually want to find him. I'm worried about how he'll look at me.

Does he understand why I didn't meet him in the stairwell? Will he even want to talk to me anymore?

The answers don't matter. We can't meet again, and the very fact that I want to is evidence that something is wrong with me. I spend every moment of every day waiting for Management to call me in for a blood test so they can uncover whatever genetic flaw makes me prone to arrogance and personal pride. To curiosity about things a gardener doesn't need to know.

My identicals seem to have no trouble keeping their thoughts on schoolwork, gardening, and winning the next field day tournament. Maybe that's because they don't know there *is* anything else to think about. If I were to tell them, would we all be so prideful and distracted? Is ignorance of our flaw the only thing keeping us all from being recalled?

If so, keeping my secret means protecting all 4,999 of my sisters.

But Poppy knows, and the only thing distracting her from her duties is concern for me.

When I'm the last one off the court after a game of indoor volleyball on a rainy afternoon, Poppy hangs back to walk with me. "Are you okay, Dahlia?" She's asked that same question a dozen times in the past few days alone.

"Yes, of course."

Her skeptical expression says she knows better, though. "Is this about the instructor position? Have you heard back yet?" My fixation on Trigger 17 makes no sense to her, so I've stopped talking to her about it. But she shares my anxiety over the thought we might be separated after graduation. "Did they select someone else?"

"I haven't heard—"

Footsteps echo toward us from the front of the building, and the precise, even cadence captures my attention. I look up and stumble over my own feet. Trigger 17 marches past my entire class without even glancing at me.

My insides are a tangle of disappointment and relief, yet I can't help turning to see where he's headed.

He gives our recreation instructor, Belay 35, a formal nod of greeting. "Your work honors us all."

"Thank you for your service." Belay 35 reciprocates the nod, and I drag my feet so I can hear. "What can I do for you, cadet?"

"Management would like to see one of your students. Dahlia 16."

My legs stop working. My feet are frozen to the floor. I've had this dream a dozen times, but suddenly it feels like a nightmare. The last thing I want is more attention from Management.

"I didn't get a ping," Belay 35 says, and I hear his athletic jacket rustle as he pulls his tablet from an inner pocket.

"They're having technical difficulties at the Management Bureau. That's why I was dispatched to deliver the message."

"What a quaint and inefficient method of communication." Belay 35 clears his throat, then raises his voice. "Dahlia 16?"

I am equal parts relieved and terrified as I turn. "Yes, sir?"

"Please report to Management immediately. I'll let Sorrel 32 know you will be delayed."

"Yes, sir."

Poppy stares at me, wide-eyed, when I fall in behind Trigger 17. She's probably wondering the same thing I am: is this about the instructor's position? Have they noticed how distracted I've become?

What kind of bitter irony is it that they would send Trigger 17 to fetch me when he is the very source of my distraction?

When we reach the common lawn, I follow him toward the gate leading out of the training ward while the rest of my class heads for our academy. As we walk, I stare at his back, noticing for the first time how much broader his shoulders are than mine. Broader even than the boys in the hydroponic gardening union. I'm so fascinated by this that I don't even realize we've turned off of the main walkway until the shadow of the Specialist Academy falls over me.

Trigger 17 has led me to the side of the building, out of sight from the common lawn, the street, and most of the nearby buildings.

I stop walking and clear my throat. "Cadet, this is not the way out of the training ward." I'm allowed to say that to him. This isn't fraternization, because he's here on official business, and that business is me. Still, I feel strangely exposed, speaking to him out loud. Outside. Where anyone could hear.

In reply he smiles and pulls open the door to his left, then motions for me to go inside.

I stare through the door at the stairwell exit of the Specialist Academy. Then I shake my head. Management is expecting me. I can't just take a detour with him!

Trigger gestures more insistently at the stairwell.

Against my better judgment, I go in. He follows me and closes the door, but before I can ask him what's going on, he gives me a "shh" gesture with one finger over his lips. Then he stares up at the series of three landings above. "Hello?"

His voice echoes, but there is no answer. We are alone.

"What are we doing here?" I demand before the echo of

his voice has fully faded from my ears. This detour *can't* be part of his official business, which means I shouldn't be talking to him. Why would he put me in this position?

"I wanted to see you," he says, as if it's just that simple, and I can't believe how casually he's willing to smash his way through the fraternization directive. "Why didn't you meet me in the dormitory stairwell?"

"Because it was too dangerous. Trigger, this is not okay!"

"But you did get my message?" he asks, as if he doesn't understand how risky it is for me to be here.

"Of course I got your message. It was wrapped around a carrot in my drawer. What was your plan? That we chat about things I'm not supposed to know on the eighteenth-floor landing?"

He shrugs. "We could have gone down to the twelfth-floor landing. That's my floor."

I'm not supposed to know what floor he lives on. We're not just breaking the fraternization directive. We're pounding it into tiny little bits.

"So was the carrot good? They're different than the ones you grow, so I wasn't sure you'd like it."

"I didn't eat it." I shake my head, trying to bring the entire preposterous, perilous conversation back on track. "I'm not a cadet. You can't just—"

"Why didn't you eat it?" He looks terribly disappointed, and in spite of the fact that we're about to be dragged away in handcuffs by soldiers, I want to fix that.

"Because . . . I wanted to keep it." The admission feels

beyond dangerous, but the lines in his forehead disappear and his bearing relaxes a little. Why does making him happy make me feel so good when we're both risking everything just by standing here?

"Oh. Well, you should probably eat it before someone finds it. There will be other carrots."

"No, there won't!" I exhale, grasping for patience. "Trigger, there can't be other carrots, and you can't sneak into my room again! You're going to get caught!"

His shrug is too casual. No matter how different his bureau is from mine, even a cadet would be punished for sneaking into a dorm room belonging to a member of another division. I'm missing something.

"I know how to avoid the cameras," he insists. "And if I have to, I can make them glitch for a second. Sometimes the feed gets fuzzy." He shrugs with a small smile. "Can't be helped."

"You . . . ?" I don't even know the word for what he's describing. "What did you do?"

"I hacked the feed," he says, and when he finds no comprehension in my expression he tries again. "I used my tablet to break into the security system—that's called hacking—and cause static in the camera feed. Just for a few seconds. It goes unnoticed because it happens periodically on its own, and since the feed isn't really down they don't send anyone to investigate."

I need a second to process what I'm hearing. I had no idea such a thing was possible. "They have a name for breaking that specific kind of rule? Maybe if they hadn't named it, you cadets wouldn't *do* it. How do you even know how to . . . hack?"

He gives me another shrug. "I'm Special Forces. My primary specialty is hand-to-hand combat, but my secondary is cyber-intelligence."

"Your instructors taught you how to bypass Lakeview's security feed?" The most daring thing I've ever done is graft a tomato vine to a potato plant and grow two kinds of vegetables from one plant.

"They taught me how to bypass *other* cities' security feeds," Trigger clarifies. "Mountainside, Oceanbay, and Valleybrook use very similar systems. From there it wasn't hard to figure out our own. They must know that's a possibility. They just don't think we'll actually do it. They have to trust us, because in a couple of years we'll be their first line of defense."

Defense against what? His training sounds more like *offense*.

Trigger's dark eyes shine even brighter for a second. "I'm the best in my class."

My gasp echoes around the stairwell.

"What?" Trigger stands straighter. "That's what this cord indicates." He tugs on the red braid looped around the stiff, square shoulder of his uniform jacket. "I'm the leader of my squad."

"Are all cadets so arrogant?" My voice is a whisper, as if volume could possibly influence the scale of my fraternization violation.

57

"That's not arrogance; it's truth."

"It's pride. What if you start fighting to bolster your own arrogance rather than to glorify and protect the city?" That would surely be a slippery slope toward ruin.

Trigger 17 looks confused. Then he chuckles. "It doesn't work like that in Defense. My 'arrogance' *does* glorify the city. And if my superior skill motivates my fellow cadets to fight harder, the city is glorified that much more."

I can hardly even process that thought. My identicals and I have spent our entire lives learning to work as a unit. To bond with and support one another without fail. To celebrate one another's successes as our own. Yet . . . "Your academy encourages competition?"

"Defense *requires* it. You can't run an army as if it's a factory, or a construction crew, or a garden. Our leaders can't be managers; they have to come from within our ranks, and command positions are awarded through competition." He takes a deep breath, then stands straighter and practically barks a motto in a practiced cadence. "It takes the best to lead the rest."

All at once I understand. But I'm not supposed to. No one outside of the Defense Bureau is supposed to know that their rules encourage competition and allow for arrogance and— evidently—for one child locking another in a dark closet.

I want to be able to declare that I'm the best hydroponic gardener in my union, but the city neither requires nor allows arrogance from its gardeners. And now I wish I didn't know that Trigger is allowed to feel and say what I am not.

"Okay. I promise I'll eat the carrot. But we have to go. I can't keep Management waiting." And I have no idea how I'll explain the delay.

Trigger 17 throws his head back and laughs. The sound echoes up through the stairwell above us, and I scowl at him. I'm not in on the joke. "Management isn't expecting you, Dahlia. I just told your instructor that so he'd let you come with me."

"You *lied* to Belay 35?" I can't even process that statement. Keeping our secret has been hard enough for me, but an outright lie? Skipping class? "What if he pings Management to verify what you told him?"

"He probably won't, because he doesn't expect to be lied to. And even if he tries, the ping won't go through, because Management's communications truly are down. I hacked the system. They're restricted to verbal communication until I repair the damage. Or until they figure out what's happened, and even if they do they can't trace it back to me."

I stare at him, wide-eyed. How can a cadet—a *student*—have broken into the city's security system without alerting the people who run that system? Just how special are these Special Forces? "Do you have any idea how insanely dangerous all this is?"

"Yes. This is what I'm trained for." Trigger looks exhilarated, and with a strange sense of intuition I realize I know exactly how he feels. This same reckless thrill races through me every time I think about him. "It's good practice for real-world application," he adds.

"But *I'm* not trained for . . . whatever this is." And all this adrenaline is making my heart race too fast.

"Relax. Once you're back in class, I'll restore Management's communications and they'll think it was a random glitch. If your friends ask what Management wanted, just tell them it was about the instructor's position, but that's all you're at liberty to say."

My focus narrows on him. "How do you know about the instructor's position?"

"It's in your file."

"You looked at my file?" Does that mean *I've* been hacked?

"How else was I supposed to know whether Management would have a plausible reason to want to see you?" Trigger gives me a sly smile. "They're very impressed with your efforts in the hydroponic lab. Your work with vines and climbers is especially noteworthy."

I shake my head, setting aside the compliment clearly meant as a distraction. "Won't they be able to see that my file was accessed?"

"Yes, if they go looking." Trigger leans against the top half of the stair rail and crosses his arms over his chest. "But I used your academic instructor's access code."

"Do I even want to know how you got that?"

His grin is small but indomitable. "Probably not."

"And you want me to lie to my friends about where I went?"

"I want you to give them the benefit of plausible deniability. Protect them from the truth, just in case. It's in everyone's best interest."

I can't argue with that.

Grasping for patience in spite of the increasingly insistent awareness that *we should not be here,* I tuck a strand of hair behind my ear and stare up at him. "Do you have an answer for everything?"

He grins. "Cadets are trained to be prepared."

I feel like I should yell at him, yet I find myself returning his smile. Something about his stalwart confidence is charming, even as it makes me want to pull my own hair out by the roots.

How is that possible? Is it something they breed into a soldier? "Are there thousands just like you?"

Finally he hesitates, clearly giving his response serious thought. "I'm not sure there are *any* like me anymore."

"What do you mean?"

"My identicals and I are genetic duplicates, of course, but that just means we're operating with the same basic genetic tools at our disposal. And obviously we've had the same training. But I'm the only one who got trapped in an elevator with a beautiful girl who so clearly wanted to ask a million questions yet so clearly knew she wasn't supposed to. My experience diverged from theirs that day. Meeting you led me and my training down a different path." He makes a gesture that encompasses the two of us. "Down *this* path."

"A path that makes you willing to break rules that Management doesn't even know it needs yet. Like 'Do not hack into the city's security and communication systems.'"

"Exactly."

What he's done is incredibly risky. Yet I understand the impulse. Before I met Trigger 17, I had no idea how little I actually knew about the world, outside of hydroponic gardening, and if that knowledge were available to me with a few taps on a tablet, as it is for him, wouldn't I tap?

Trigger pushes himself away from the stairs and stands straighter. "I'm sorry for all the covert maneuvers. I just wanted to talk to you again, and this seemed simpler than rigging an elevator to break down while we're both on it. Although I have to admit, that was my backup plan."

"I can't tell whether you're joking." Violet is like that. It drives me nuts.

"I am. Mostly. Although it is much harder to find time to talk to you than to girls from my own union."

"Girls from . . . ?" My chest aches in an entirely new and painful way. We're allowed to talk to the boys in our union, so why does the thought of him talking to the girls in his union make me feel a little mad and a little sick at the same time?

"If . . ." I can't figure out how to ask what I want to know. "If you weren't supposed to talk to those girls, would you go through this much trouble? Would you break rules for them?"

Trigger is silent while he thinks, and each second that passes without an answer makes my heart beat harder. Finally, his head tilts to the side and he looks down at me with somber consideration. "It's possible that I made hacking into Management's communication system sound easier than it was. It actually took me a week and a half to analyze and break down the process, and another couple of days to work up the nerve to try it. I don't think I would have done that for anyone else, Dahlia. I'm not even sure I did it for you. This was kind of selfish. I wanted to see you. I wanted to talk to you. I wanted to know if you liked the carrot, and I wanted to tell you about where I found it and how it was growing."

Now my heart is beating too hard for an entirely different, equally perplexing reason.

"Why?" Why would he be willing to take such risks for me? If it had been one of my identicals trapped with him in that elevator, would he have gone through so much trouble to talk to her, or would he and that hypothetical identical simply have parted ways after the elevator incident and gone about their separate lives?

Why are Trigger and I still thinking about each other six weeks later?

"Because you spoke to me."

"Because I . . . ?"

"In the elevator. You were as scared of talking to me—of breaking a rule—as you were of plummeting to your death. But you did it. A *lot*. You're like a pretty little hydroponic flower, but you have wild roots. Dahlia, you look like a gardener, but you *feel* like a fighter."

Something deep inside me stirs. Something . . . hungry.

We're only a couple of feet apart—even closer than we were in the elevator—and I have a sudden inexplicable urge to close the distance between us. To touch him.

I've never wanted to touch any of the boys in my union. That impulse seems very strange. Yet it doesn't feel wrong.

63

"What?" Trigger has noticed me staring. "Is there something on my face?" He runs one hand over his jawline, and it makes a soft scratching sound against the short stubble on his chin.

"No. Well, I mean it looks like you need to shave, and I . . ." I can't look away.

One corner of his mouth turns up and I suddenly feel like he can see right through my skull into my most private thoughts. "You want to feel it?"

"I don't . . . I couldn't . . ." If there are rules against talking to members of other divisions, there *must* be rules against touching members of other divisions. Yet I can't think of any, probably because it never occurred to Management that we would try.

I mean, we'd have to be *looking* for trouble, right?

"I can't . . ."

Trigger takes my hand, and my heart leaps into my throat. I've never touched a boy before. His hand is warm but not really soft. There is a thick bit of scar tissue on his thumb, and I can't resist moving my finger over the smooth lump.

I look up and his gaze captures mine. All the warmth from his hand rushes through me and settles into my face. Touching him is one thing, but *watching* him while we're touching feels somehow both prohibited and familiar. Forbidden and intimate in a way I've never considered before.

Trigger lifts my hand toward his face and I suck in a deep breath. He smiles as if the sound means something to him. Something he likes very much. He presses my fingertips against the back of his jaw, just below his ear, and I'm surprised by how stiff the stubble is there. How coarse.

He drags my hand slowly down his jaw toward his chin, and the sensation is prickly but warm. The combination is strangely enthralling. It's so different from anything I've ever felt. So rough and—

My fingers slide over his bottom lip, and the transition between rough and soft is so jarring I'm almost startled by it. So startled that I don't even realize at first that his hand is gone. I'm in charge of my fingers, and they seem to have found his mouth on their own.

I look up until my gaze meets his again. I can't make sense of the intense look in his eyes, but it makes my flush deepen. His pupils are dilated. His breathing has become slow and deep.

Then I realize I'm still touching his lip.

I jerk my hand away and smooth my hair back from my forehead, trying to disguise my embarrassment.

"So?" Trigger asks. "Does it feel like you expected?"

"I don't know what I expected." I don't know how to look at him anymore after having lost control of my own hand.

"It will feel different in the morning. After I shave," he says, and despite my ironclad certainty that it will never be possible, I want to feel that too.

"We have to go. I have to get back before . . ." Before I lose all ability to function. "Before someone figures out what we're doing."

What *are* we doing? Is it so terrible to want to know what

beard stubble feels like? Is this more evidence of a genetic flaw, or would any girl do the same thing, given the opportunity?

It's easy to follow the rules when you're never given an opportunity to break them.

Maybe I'm not flawed. Trigger attributes his misbehavior not to a genetic flaw but to experiences he's had that his identicals have not. Could that be true for me?

No. Cadets are designed with different genetic traits than laborers are. He's supposed to react differently in any given situation than I am.

So why do I understand everything he's told me? Why do I not just comprehend it but *feel* it?

There is something seriously wrong with me. I am *dangerously* flawed, and every moment I spend here with him is another moment I'm putting my sisters' lives at risk. *Poppy's* life.

"Trigger, I . . ."

He steps closer, and his proximity steals the words from my tongue. If I inhale too deeply, we will be touching. "Yes, Dahlia?"

I can feel the heat radiating from his body. He's so close that I have to look up to see his face. "We have to go. Promise me you'll never do this again. For both our sakes. For our identicals' sakes."

"You're really scared." His smile fades with the realization, and the heat in his eyes cools. "I was very careful, Dahlia. No one will know about the hacking, and unless you tell them, no one will know about this stairwell."

I believe him. I can see that the last thing he wants is to put me in danger. But things are different for me in a way he clearly can't understand. I am rarely ever without the company of my classmates, and every moment that I am draws notice. Management doesn't want laborers to know things we don't need to know, because that will distract us from our purpose. I've seen that very clearly over the past few weeks.

Management is right.

This is wrong.

"Promise me, Trigger 17."

Finally he nods. "I promise. But I can't promise I won't look for you."

I don't argue, because I can't promise him the same thing. "I think looking is okay, as long as no one notices. But this is not."

He nods again and takes a step back, putting more air between us. More distance. But his gaze has snagged on my mouth. My attention is drawn to his lips too, just as my fingers were. I'm not surprised by that, but I can't articulate why. I can't explain my growing fascination with his mouth.

"We should go. Separately."

He looks disappointed, but he agrees. So I take a deep breath and try to swallow my own disappointment over how very final my exit feels. Then I step out of the stairwell and close the door at my back. And I walk away from Trigger 17 again.

SIX

I report to my gardening unit still wearing my athletic clothing, and Sorrel 32 gives me twenty minutes to return to my room to shower and change clothes. As I jog down the winding sidewalk through the common lawn, I notice that every group I pass turns to look at me. They're not staring, exactly. They don't seem suspicious or worried. They're just curious because I am alone.

The fact that being alone no longer bothers me makes me very nervous. Someone is bound to notice eventually.

Alone in my dorm room, I take a clean change of clothes into the bathroom, careful to grab the lumpy shirt. While the shower runs, I remove Trigger's carrot from the folded bundle and stare at it. It no longer smells like dirt, yet it still smells . . . earthy. It's a different scent than that of a hydroponically grown carrot, maybe because it isn't a variety we grow in class. Maybe because it wasn't carefully engineered, fertilized, and monitored.

Now that I know I have to eat the carrot, I can't figure out how I ever resisted in the first place.

I break off the fibrous cord at the end, then bite off the tip and chew it slowly. The flavor and texture don't seem to have suffered after more than fourteen days in my dry, clean drawer. Though it has a wilder taste and a stringier texture than the cultivated carrots we grow in class, it is not woody or tough. The carrot is an interesting mixture of sweet and bitter, and I wish I could taste it steamed with a little salt. Or sautéed with butter and onion. Or glazed and baked.

It doesn't seem fair that those of us who grow food for the city will never have a chance to prepare it.

On the first truly cool day of fall, Belay 35, our athletic instructor, decides that the year-sixteen hydroponic gardening classes—both male and female—should enjoy the beautiful weather by spending our recreation hour outside. I'm thrilled by this idea until it becomes clear that by "enjoy the beautiful weather," he means "jog laps around the training ward."

Jogging is my least favorite form of exercise. Except for running.

But it *is* a beautiful day, so I grab a bottle full of cold water and file in line between Poppy and Sorrel and next to a boy named Indigo 16.

"It seems like you're gone all the time now," Sorrel calls softly from behind me as we take off down the sidewalk at a comfortable pace.

"She's only been called out twice," Poppy says over her shoulder. "Let's keep that in perspective."

She doesn't mention the times I've returned to the dormitory alone to change.

"What's it like, leaving the training ward on your own?" Violet asks from behind Sorrel as we pass the Workforce Academy, where a line of female mechanics in gray coveralls are filing through the front door.

"It's . . . uncomfortable." The lie tastes bitter, but Trigger's right. It's necessary. "It makes me feel exposed. As if it's cold outside and I forgot my coat."

Poppy shudders. "You'll have to get used to that if you become an instructor, but I'm glad it's you and not me. We were never meant to make our way alone."

I can't shake the feeling that she's right, but not for the reason she means. Trigger and I have nothing genetic in common, yet I feel anything but alone when I'm with him.

As our pace picks up and talking becomes uncomfortable, I watch Indigo 16 and his classmates jogging in the line next to ours. He and his identicals are an inch or so taller than my sisters and I are, yet a good six inches shorter than Trigger 17. The gardening boys have narrower, longer faces than Trigger and much less facial stubble, even though it's late afternoon.

Indigo 16 and his identicals also have narrower shoulders

and chests, and though—like us—they are fit from lifting jugs of fertilizer and from an hour a day spent in recreation, they are not as obviously strong as any of the cadets. Not as solid.

Trigger's face flashes through my memory as I run, and my sudden warmth doesn't seem related to exertion.

Each genome is unique and no two classes can look alike, because of the Preservation and Equal Distribution of Genetic Traits directive. But I can't help wondering why geneticists would bother with other male genomes after Trigger 17's was created.

His form is clearly a triumph of genetic design, and I can't imagine how future efforts could possibly improve upon it.

Or am I being unfair to the other boys?

Why do I prefer Trigger's physical form? Why should I have any preference at all?

As we jog, I watch the pendulum motion of Poppy's ponytail. I'm dying to ask her which she prefers, but I'm pretty sure my sisters have never truly noticed the boys in our division, much less boys in other divisions, and asking the question will only show them how different I've really become.

As we pass the Specialist Academy, my thoughts wander to the stairwell where I touched Trigger's face. Ahead is the Art Academy, where—

Motion in my peripheral vision draws my gaze, and I slow just a little when I notice two identical female soldiers standing next to a patrol car that has stopped in the middle of the road. Rather than the typical uniform, the soldiers are wearing all black, and one of them is gesturing angrily to a girl on the curving sidewalk. Though I can't hear what she's saying, it's clear that she wants the girl to get into the car.

I don't recognize the girl's uniform either. Her pants are blue and formfitting, and her shirt is a pale red color that I can't associate with any bureau. Before I've gotten more than a glance at her, one of the soldiers pushes her into the back of the car and slams the door.

Why is the girl alone? Where are the soldiers taking her, and why would she resist when disobeying an order is grounds for a DNA analysis in search of genetic flaws?

The soldiers slide into the front seats, and as the vehicle begins to roll forward along the cruise strip painted on the road I see the girl's angry pout in profile. I don't recognize her genome. She has olive-toned skin and dark hair worn longer than is considered practical for either Workforce or Defense.

Maybe she's Management. We don't have much contact with the managers in training, except when they get to practice bossing us around, so she probably belongs to a class I've never noticed before. And who, other than Management, would dare argue with a soldier?

I face forward again to see if anyone else noticed the incident, but the rest of my class is staring at something else.

A crowd of people has gathered in front of the Defense Academy, but they seem to be standing in very neatly ordered rows. A few steps later I understand why: the crowd is made up of soldiers—not cadets—and they are standing in formation, in full uniform.

Hundreds of them. Maybe thousands.

Belay 35 slows, and we slow with him until we're just standing on the sidewalk. Staring. "Everyone take a short breather and drink some water," Belay 35 calls out without even looking back at us.

For a moment no one moves. We never take a break until we've completed the first circuit of the training ward, and when we do rest, we take our pulses and wait for Belay 35 to record them on his tablet.

This is not right.

Our neat lines sluggishly collapse into confused clusters, and I notice that even though there's no rule against it, our cliques do not cross the gender line. As if the girls and guys have no interest in talking to one another.

"Why are there so many soldiers at the academy?" Violet asks as she twists open the valve on her bottle. "Some kind of training exercise?"

Poppy wipes a drip of water from her chin. "Do graduates still do training exercises?"

I don't know. In fact, I have no idea what cadets do after they become full-fledged soldiers, beyond their general mission to protect and defend. I make a mental note to ask Trigger—

No. I can't ask Trigger anything, because we can never be alone again.

Why is that so hard for me to remember?

"Class!" Belay 35 calls, and we turn as one, all conversation fading into attentive silence. "Stay here and rest for a minute. I'll be right back." Without waiting to make sure his directions will be heeded—there's little doubt of that—our instructor jogs toward the Defense Academy.

"That's weird," Sorrel says as we watch him go, and I hear the same sentiment echoed from the other students around us. I've never seen an instructor so obviously curious about what's going on in another division, which is definitely none of his business. Yet Belay 35 is clearly headed toward the Defense Academy for some answers.

"There are more coming," Poppy says, staring over my shoulder, and I turn to see a large group of soldiers jogging in formation across the common lawn, their uniforms crisply pressed, their footsteps muffled by the grass beneath their feet. Each soldier carries a black duffel bag over one shoulder and a rifle held at an angle in front of his chest.

Violet shields the sun from her eyes with one hand. "They look kind of young."

I glance at the soldiers, and the rest of the world seems to go dark around me. All the boys have Trigger's face.

But year seventeen hasn't graduated yet. They can't wear soldiers' uniforms. They're still cadets.

Terrified, I spin again to squint at those already in formation in front of the Defense Academy, and my worst fear is confirmed. Those soldiers—both male and female—are also from year seventeen.

"They're graduating . . . ," I mumble. Trigger will be moving to the residential ward, and even once I graduate our paths will likely never cross. He'll be sent farther into the

74

wild than ever before, and for longer than ever before. Should Lakeview go to war, he will fight. He might die.

I will never see Trigger 17 again.

"They can't be graduating. Defense doesn't graduate until December," one of the boys says from a clique near ours. "This is nearly three months early."

"Well, yesterday they were cadets and today they're clearly soldiers," Sorrel says. "What's your explanation?"

He frowns. "I don't know."

"We're not supposed to know," the boy next to him adds, and I see with a glance at his jacket that this is Indigo, who's been jogging next to me for ten minutes.

"Obviously." Poppy rolls her eyes. "But if this weren't out of the ordinary, Belay 35 wouldn't . . ."

The discussion dies as our focus is pulled back to our instructor, who's now speaking to the instructor of another class, which has also stopped to watch. Poppy's right. Belay 35 wouldn't make such a production of his curiosity if what we're seeing wasn't frighteningly abnormal.

Why would Lakeview graduate a class of Defense cadets three months early?

Belay 35 returns and orders us back into two lines. He doesn't offer us any information, and I can't tell whether any was offered to him.

The only person I know who will have the answer and be willing to share it with me is somewhere in that formation of graduating cadets, about to be marched out of my life forever.

I will never know why.

75

SEVEN

For days, I scan the face of every soldier I see, hoping against all odds that somehow Trigger 17's squad was assigned to patrol the training ward after graduation. The chances of that are slim for a Special Forces unit, yet I can't stop hoping.

But none of the soldiers I see around the common lawn are wearing Trigger's face, and none of the remaining cadets are older than year sixteen. A week after the unexpected graduation, I force myself to face the reality that Trigger is gone.

Which is why, a few weeks after I've mentally said goodbye to him, I am stunned to step out of the Workforce Academy for our monthly field day and find Trigger 17 looking right at me. Wearing a cadet's recreation uniform.

I can tell it's him even without the red braid, and even though I'm not close enough to see the scar on his forearm. I can see it in the way he watches me, even though I look just like all the other girls pouring out of the academy onto the lawn.

He's in the company of five of his identicals, forming a squad of six charged with overseeing a competition where several dozen year-fifteen cadets spar one-on-one in the center of a circle formed by their peers. The year seventeens are acting as both judges and mentors, and their instructor appears to be evaluating their performance in both regards as he taps on his tablet.

Time seems to hang suspended between us while Trigger and I stare at each other, but I know that mere seconds have passed when Poppy passes me on her way down the steps toward our first event without even noticing my hesitation.

"Hey." I jog to catch up with her. "Aren't those year-seventeen cadets from the division that graduated last month?" Can she see what I'm seeing, or am I imagining the whole thing?

Poppy follows my gaze, and her groan is proof enough. "Yeah. I guess they didn't all graduate."

I'm so relieved that I let out a breath I didn't even realize I was holding.

"But, Dahlia, you have to forget about him and your weird fascination," she whispers as she tugs me onto the cool fall grass. "He's probably long gone."

I don't argue with her for the same reason I didn't tell her about talking to Trigger in the stairwell. Poppy is my *best friend.* She's the last person in the world I'd want to burden with such dangerous knowledge.

She deserves nothing less than absolute ignorance of whatever genetic flaw we carry.

"Why would the city graduate only part of a division?" I ask instead.

Poppy shrugs. "Why would they graduate that part of a division three months early? Who knows why Management does what it does? All I know is that it's none of our business. Come on." She takes off toward the common lawn, where our identicals are already setting up sporting equipment and dividing into teams under the supervision of Belay 35 and a few other athletic instructors. All the male year-thirty-five instructors look just like Belay, but there are several other genomes from other years represented as well.

Between rounds of volleyball, soccer, and relay races, I stare at the cadets across the common lawn, but over that distance I can't tell which of the black-clad bodies and dark-eyed gazes belongs to Trigger 17. Yet for the first time I notice the difference between our recreation and his.

Workforce's athletic activities consist exclusively of team sports. Yet while the cadets cheer for one another and shout advice as their classmates grapple, their activities invariably pit one cadet against another. Their races aren't relays. They play tennis one-on-one. They compete for the most accurate target shooting. Their efforts—both their successes and failures—stand on their own.

I'm not sure their way is better than ours, but I'm not sure it's worse either. I think it's just different. And I'm amazed that I've never noticed that before.

After my leg of the sprint relay, I look up to find that the cadets' exercise has ended and the last of the year fifteens are filing back toward their academy. Their year-seventeen mentors are nowhere to be seen.

I can't set aside my disappointment even when Violet smacks me on the shoulder with the baton she has just carried across the finish line, earning our team the relay championship. Our victory cupcakes taste bittersweet, even though chocolate is my favorite flavor. I hardly hear our athletic instructor's speech lauding our teamwork and dedication to the group effort rather than individual glory.

When Belay 35 asks for a volunteer to return the sporting equipment to the utility shed behind our academy, I raise my hand. I need a few minutes to myself to process the knowledge that Trigger 17 isn't gone. Not yet, anyway. So I put the baton tape in my pocket, throw the mesh bag full of balls over my left shoulder, and tuck the bundle of relay batons under my right arm. Then I head for the back of the building in spite of my instructor's surprise that I haven't chosen an identical to help me.

In the utility shed, I place the volleyballs and soccer balls on their designated racks and toss the empty mesh bag into a basket full of others just like it. I'm counting the relay batons to make sure they've all been recovered when the door at my back closes.

I gasp and whirl around. The batons clatter to the ground, and one of them hits my foot. I can't make out anything in the darkness, and I can't remember where the light switch is.

"Dahlia. It's me."

I don't recognize Trigger 17 by his voice. I recognize him by the warmth in the way he says my name. By the casual nature of his declaration, as if we can simply pick up where we left off. As if the entire world isn't just beyond that closed door, waiting for proof that we are both flawed. That we shouldn't even exist.

"I thought you were gone with the rest of your division," I say into the darkness. "What are you still doing here?"

"Gone with . . . ? Oh, the graduates?" His silhouette shrugs against the greater darkness. "Those were infantry cadets. Around three thousand of them total. There are about a thousand of us left, and we're all specialists. Linguists. Explosives experts. Special Forces."

"Why did the infantry graduate early?"

"Who knows? I guess Lakeview needed some more grunts."

"But they didn't finish training, did they?"

"*We're* not quite finished." His shadow lays one hand over its heart, a movement I can hardly make out in the dark. "But it doesn't take a lot of training to catch a bullet."

"Why would the city need more infantry if we're not at war? We're not, are we?"

Trigger's shadow shrugs. "Not that I know of. I've been in the wild for nearly a month, and the only thing I know right now is that I want to see you."

He steps forward, and I lose my breath.

"What are you doing?" I can't tell if my pulse is racing

from the scare he's just given me, from the fact that he hasn't graduated and left me, or from the knowledge that we're alone in the dark. Or because now I might get to touch him again. Is it early enough in the day for his face to be smooth?

Does he want me to touch him?

It doesn't matter. As happy as I am to see him, we can't be here. Even if Special Forces cadets are afforded some measure of freedom while they're not in class, I'm not. My instructor will be expecting me.

"I brought you something." There's a new note in his voice—an eager excitement. He sounds like I feel when it's time to clean out the water bed and plant something brand-new. "I saw you come in here alone, and I thought this would be my best chance to give it to you. This shed could be our new stairwell."

I swallow the lump in my throat and remind myself to breathe. That last sentence made no sense, yet I understand it perfectly.

He steps closer, and I can see him better now that my eyes have adjusted to the low light. He's holding something small and vaguely oblong between his left index finger and thumb, and I wonder if his genome is left-handed. Then I notice that what he's holding has a familiar silhouette.

I squint in the darkness. "Is that . . . ?"

"It's a peanut. I pulled the plant out of the ground yesterday afternoon, about halfway between Lakeview and Riverbend, and I saved this one for you." He drops the peanut in my cupped palm, and I lift it to my face for a better look. It

smells like the earth. There are still tiny clumps of dirt clinging to the shell.

Somehow, like the carrot, this wild peanut seems . . .
hardy. It must be, to have survived out there on its own with
no one feeding or watering it, or monitoring its health, the
efficiency of its growth, or the state of its environment.

"Should I eat it?"

He laughs. "That's typically what one does with a peanut."

"But once I eat it, it will be gone."

"And as with the carrot, there will be others, Dahlia. I
know where to look."

But he shouldn't have a chance to bring me another peanut, because we're not supposed to be alone together. We're
not supposed to be talking. I can't think of a rule specifically
forbidding bringing wild produce into the city, but I'm pretty
sure he would get in trouble for it if anyone knew.

Yet somehow I believe him. There will be other peanuts.

So I crack the shell in one hand and pull the top half off.
Lying in the cradle of the bottom half are three round kernels, which he would probably call nuts. They are perfectly
formed and covered in a thin reddish skin. Though it was
grown without fertilizer, constant attention, or proper spac-
ing, I see no obvious flaws in this wild peanut.

I dump the kernels into my palm, then toss all three into
my mouth.

Trigger 17 watches me while I chew, and to my surprise I
can actually taste a difference between this wild peanut and
the ones we're served as high-protein snacks. Maybe it's a dif-

ferent variety. Or maybe different growth methods yield different tastes. Either way I am fascinated. I want to see where this peanut grew. I want to see *how* it grew.

I want to know if peanuts that grow all on their own, with no one micromanaging their environment, can possibly be as strong as peanuts grown side by side in a bed of thousands under ideal circumstances.

But those are things I was never meant to know.

Trigger 17 is someone I was never meant to know, and we should not be here. Especially considering that he's had no chance to hack into any system to buy us time.

"I have to be showered and back at my desk in twenty minutes." Yet I can hear the reluctance in my own voice.

He takes another step toward me. "How fast can you shower?" His voice is suddenly deep and gravelly, and the question sends an unexpected bolt of anticipation through me that settles low in my stomach.

"I . . ." My whole body seems to be tingling, and I don't know why.

"I haven't stopped thinking about you," he whispers, and I am relieved to realize I'm not the only one haunted by our stolen time in the stairwell. "When I eat, I wonder if you grew the food. When I see a flower, I wonder if it's a dahlia. Nothing has changed that I can tell, yet everything feels different. It's like you're on the edge of my vision everywhere I go, but when I turn to look you're never there."

I take a deep breath, but immediately I need another. I've felt the same way for weeks. "Why?" I ask him in spite of the now-familiar flush in my cheeks. "Why can't I get you out of my head?"

What is this feeling? Why am I drawn to him like a magnet to metal, when I know this can only mean trouble for us both? Management makes no effort to keep the boys and girls in the Workforce Academy apart, but we aren't even allowed to speak to people from other bureaus. Is this why?

"Because you're attracted to me." Trigger's gaze seems to see deep inside me. "And it's very much mutual."

"I don't understand what that means." But maybe I do, at least a little bit. My hands feel pulled to his flesh—to his arms, his chest. My gaze feels pulled to his face, where it snags on his mouth again, even in the dark.

"I know. Workforce doesn't truly fraternize. You girls exist alongside the boys in your union, but it's like you're uninterested in each other, and I can't figure out why. Unless it's that the boys in your union don't look very different from the girls."

"Is it different in Defense? Is your fraternizing more like . . . this? This attraction?" I want him to say yes, because that would mean that what's considered a flaw in me isn't considered a flaw in *every* girl. That would make me feel a little less damaged. Yet I want him to say no, because I don't want to think about Trigger 17 feeling this strange and electrifying attraction to some other girl.

"Yes. Every time we leave the city, we're risking our lives. In order to stay functional and efficient under that kind of pressure, we're allowed to decompress on a level commensurate with our stress level. That's true for both our male and female cadets."

I frown at him in the dark. "I only understood about half of that." But the parts I understand have deepened the warmth spreading through me.

The only basis I know of for boys and girls being drawn to each other comes from a now-obsolete biological imperative my class learned about in our basic biology unit from year fifteen.

Much like plants growing in the dirt, people used to grow in the wild as well. Children were produced one at a time, with only the occasional set of two or three, and even those rarely matched one another. Fertilization was messy and ridiculously inefficient. The process required a man and a woman, rather than a geneticist and a lab, and conception was never a guarantee, but because that was primitive mankind's only way to reproduce, men and women were drawn to each other for the purpose of procreation.

The whole thing was crude and uncivilized, yet neither of those adjectives seems to apply to the way I feel with Trigger staring down at me. I feel like my heart is too big for its cavity and my skin is too flushed to be at a normal temperature.

This isn't supposed to be happening. Mankind has moved beyond the need for such urges and biological reactions. Yet Trigger doesn't seem surprised or confused.

"I'll show you." He takes another step toward me. "May I kiss you?"

"Kiss . . . ?" My question dies on my tongue as his hands land on my shoulders and slide down my arms. He bends toward me and I suck in a surprised breath. Then his lips meet mine, and I lose the ability to think. I can only feel, and I've never felt anything like this in my life.

This is not a kiss. A kiss is bestowed upon skinned knees by nannies in the primary dorm. A kiss is bestowed upon cheeks by identicals in celebration of a team victory. A kiss eases the perception of pain or elevates a feeling of success. This is something else entirely.

This kiss ignites the heat simmering low in my stomach like a match dropped in a puddle of fuel.

Trigger sucks gently on my lower lip, and my mouth opens in surprise. He slides one hand into my hair, tilting my head for a better angle, and I feel the gentle graze of his teeth. The tip of his tongue brushes my upper lip, then dips into my mouth, and my world explodes into a vibrancy and intensity I have never imagined possible.

When Trigger steps back, he leaves me gasping for breath. Hungry for more. "That's a kiss," he whispers.

Though my sixteen years of life experience argue otherwise, I am suddenly certain that he's right. That I've been tragically misled on the subject. "Show me again."

He reaches for me, a wicked smile haunting his mouth in the darkness. We are deep in the middle of our second kiss when the door flies open. Harsh daylight drenches our private moment. Terror surges through me.

Belay 35 stands in the doorway. At his back are two identical soldiers from year twenty-two. "Dahlia 16!" my instructor cries as the soldiers push past him.

"No! Wait!" Trigger shouts as they haul him away from me. "This isn't her fault. I snuck into the shed. I did this."

I hear a soft zipping sound as they secure his hands at his back with a plastic strip.

"You are both hereby remanded to the custody of Management for violation of the fraternization directive," one of the soldiers informs us.

My heart races as they turn me around and push me up against the volleyball rack. Several of the balls fall and bounce at my feet. One of the soldiers pulls my hands behind me while the other slips a zip restraint over them. The plastic pins my wrists together and pinches my skin, but I don't truly understand the meaning of words like *fear* and *humiliation* until they haul me out of the shed.

A class of female year-sixteen carpenters watches from the lawn, their soccer game forgotten. They stare at me, shocked, their expressions an exact reflection of the fear my own must show, because we all share the same face.

No, we share much more than that. If something is wrong with me, it's wrong with them too. They know what my arrest means as well as I do.

As the soldiers haul me down the curving sidewalk toward the gate leading out of the training ward, the athletic instructors begin to round up the soccer players, herding several dozen of my terrified identicals toward the academy to await instructions from Management.

Other groups of identicals stop walking, running relays, and weeding flower beds to stare at me with detached fascination. My arrest is no threat to those who don't share my face.

I don't know where they've taken Trigger. The only thing I know for sure is that I've managed to stand out from my peers again. But this time I've become a spectacle. I am clearly defective.

And the world has no place for defects.

EIGHT

The patrol car rolls to a stop in front of the Management Bureau, and one of the soldiers helps me out of the back-seat because my hands are still bound. Without a word, they march me into the lobby, and people turn to look. I stare at the ground. My face burns hotter with every step. Cady 34 was right—I was not meant to be anything more than a single pixel out of a much greater image.

I was never meant to be noticed on my own.

We head through the shiny lobby to the very elevator Trigger 17 and I shared weeks before, but if the soldiers are aware of the coincidence, I can't tell. I think about that day as the elevator climbs, and even now I can't truly regret speaking to Trigger. When the doors slide open on the top floor, the soldiers pull me along too fast for me to read any of the signs.

I have no idea what office takes up the fourteenth floor of the Management Bureau.

The soldiers march me down several hallways and through several doors they have to access by scanning the bar codes on their wrists. Each door leads to another hallway lined with more closed doors. This place is a maze.

The rooms are neither labeled nor numbered, and that fact makes my chest feel tight. Without signs and placards, how can anyone know what kind of work goes on here? How can people know whether they are in the right place?

Are we not supposed to know those things?

Finally I am led into an open area from which several hallways branch. The soldiers guide me down the first hall on the left, and one of them holds his wrist beneath a sensor built into the door. A light flashes green and the door unlocks with the whisper of a sliding bolt.

"Hold out your hand," one of the soldiers says as he slices through the plastic loop binding my wrists. He pulls a pen-shaped object from one pocket, and my pulse jumps. I try to withdraw my hand, but the other soldier seizes my wrist. His grip is fierce and bruising. My heart beats so hard my ribs hurt.

This is my worst nightmare.

"I'm not defective." I know that's a lie, but terror has stolen my courage. With a soul-shattering bolt of shock, I realize I don't want to die, even though my death would benefit Lakeview. I don't want Poppy or any of the other girls wearing my face to die. I would rather have them around me—flaws and all—than give them up for the good of the city.

For the first time in my life, I do not care about the welfare of the city that created me and gave me life. That raised and educated me. The city I was intended to serve since before I was even a handful of carefully designed cells.

The first soldier presses the pen to the pad of my right index finger and again I try to pull away, but my struggle is useless. He pushes a button on top of the pen. A needle shoots from the bottom into my skin. The sting is slight, but it echoes through me like a mortal wound.

As he releases the depressor, the needle sucks up several drops of blood so my genome can be examined for flaws. The soldier releases my arm and shoves me into the room they've just unlocked, and before I can even take a deep breath they've closed the door behind me.

The bolt slides into place, and a chill crawls across my skin.

The soldiers' footsteps get softer as they walk away, and I spin to stare through the window in the door. The hallway is deserted. There are several other closed doors with identical glass windows, but the rooms I can see into are all dark and evidently empty.

My room is empty too, except for me. There is no carpet and no furniture. The walls, floor, ceiling, and door are all made of the same smooth material, and every surface is painted the same pale gray. The consistency is disorienting.

I can't tell where the floor ends and the walls begin until I'm practically standing in the corner.

This room feels like it can't truly exist, and in it I feel like I don't exist either. Maybe that's intentional. To get me used to the inevitability of what's coming.

Defective and inefficient genomes must be recalled for the good of the city. That is the most fundamental principle of a productive and orderly society. There hasn't been a recall in my lifetime, but I've always known it could happen. I've always known it *should* happen if Lakeview were ever burdened with a flawed genome.

What I didn't know is how terrified the defective identicals would feel. How reluctant they would be to give up their lives—to simply cease existing—for the good of the city.

I never imagined that selfless commitment could feel so terrifying.

Footsteps clack from outside my door, and I press my face against the window—the only feature in this strange gray room. On the other side of the glass, two more soldiers escort a man in a white lab coat toward the room across the hall. His eyes are brown, like mine, and his hair is just starting to turn gray, but his face is unlined. I've never seen his genome before, but the lab coat can mean only one thing: he is a scientist. From the Specialist Bureau.

The soldiers unlock the door, and as they push the man into the room he twists to argue with them, gripping the doorjamb desperately. The name embroidered on the left side of his lab coat is Wexler 42.

The door closes, framing his face in a square of glass, and Wexler's focus finds me. He goes still as the soldiers walk away, leaving us staring at each other. Wexler frowns, studying my features. Then recognition hits him and he stumbles back from the door, wide-eyed.

He knows me. Or at least, he knows my face.

It's no surprise that he might have seen one—or more likely a pair—of my identicals somewhere around the city, even outside the training ward. There are five thousand of us, after all. But why does he seem so shocked? Why does looking at me so clearly terrify him?

Wexler steps forward again until his nose is nearly pressed against the glass. He studies what he can see of my features, and the intensity of his focus draws chills across my arms.

Finally, he blinks and steps back from the window again. His cell door opens. Just an inch at first. But when no alarm sounds and no footsteps come running, he pushes the door the rest of the way open.

I stare, stunned. How has he . . . ?

My gaze catches on the doorjamb, and I see a strip of white over the hole, which has prevented the latch from sliding into place and locking. It's some kind of tape, which he obviously pressed into place during his struggle with the soldiers. Did he grab it on the way out of his lab when the soldiers came for him? How did he know he would need it?

Wexler 42 steps into the hallway and glances in both directions, his frame tense. He's ready to run.

Instead he crosses the hall toward me. A light flashes green over my door and he pulls it open; he's unlocked my cell with the bar code on his wrist. Scientists evidently have very high security clearances.

Wexler and I stare at each other, this time with no glass between us. A small smile haunts his mouth as he studies my face.

I don't realize I'm holding my breath until I try to speak. "Who—" I inhale and try again. "Who are you?" I whisper.

"I'm the man who got you into this."

"What? I don't understand." Trigger 17 got me into this. I got *myself* into this.

The scientist's gaze drops to the embroidery on the front of my jacket. "Dahlia." He says my name as if he's tasting it. Then he looks right into my eyes and whispers one more word. "*Run.*"

Wexler 42 turns, and his footsteps whisper down the hall, opposite the direction the soldiers went in.

My stomach flip-flops. I catch the door before it can close and stick my head into the hall in time to see him disappear behind a door labeled with an image of a staircase.

Wexler 42 is gone, and my cell is unlocked.

My legs itch to move, but what good would running do? I have nowhere to go. But if I'm here when they find whatever genetic flaw is swimming around in my DNA, I will be euthanized along with my identicals for the good of the city.

Before I can decide what to do, loud footsteps echo toward me, accompanied by voices.

Panicked, I reach into my pocket and am relieved to find

the roll of baton tape still there. I tear off a piece and use it like Wexler did to keep my door from latching as I ease it silently, carefully closed.

The steps and voices come closer. Another soldier appears in the hallway with a man in a suit and tie. The name tag pinned over his suit jacket pocket reads FORD 45, MANAGEMENT BUREAU CHIEF.

He is in charge of the entire Management Bureau. Which means he answers only to the Administrator.

When Ford sees that the room across from mine is empty, his face turns an alarming shade of red. "Send out an alert ping for Wexler 42 to all patrol units," the manager barks. "Include his genome code and a photograph, but withhold all other specifics. And strip his clearance," he orders.

The soldier pulls a small tablet from his pocket and begins typing on it, and I understand that the scientist's bar code won't unlock any more doors for either of us.

"And get Wexler's supervisor in here to explain what we're dealing with," Ford 45 adds. "All that 'helix' and 'allele' talk from the genetics lab sounds like nonsense to me."

Genetics lab? Wexler is a *geneticist*? Why would Management detain a geneticist within minutes of my arrest?

Ford turns to study me through the window in my door, but based on the utter lack of emotion he may as well be looking at a piece of furniture. Then he marches down the hall again, with the soldier on his heels, still tapping and swiping on his tablet. Just before they move out of earshot, I hear Ford say, "If I don't know exactly what's wrong with her in ten minutes, you'll be scrubbing toilets in the barracks for the rest of your life."

My pulse races so fast the small room begins to spin around me. I sink onto my heels to keep from falling.

Wexler isn't just *a* geneticist. He's *my* geneticist. The scientist who designed my genome. Management took him into custody in case they find a flaw in my DNA, which he will be held accountable for.

Which five thousand of my identicals—including me—will be recalled for.

I'm the man who got you into this.

Suddenly his declaration makes a certain strange sense.

Why would Wexler run unless he *already* knows what the genetic exam will uncover? Why would he tell *me* to run unless he knows we're both about to be recalled?

Something *is* wrong with me, and the only man who knows what that is has just fled for his life.

And given me the opportunity to run for mine.

Heart pounding, I push my cell door open and peek into the hall. When I'm sure it's empty, I run for the stairs as quickly and quietly as I can.

The door to the stairwell closes behind me with a soft whoosh of air, and the sudden silence around me is unnerving. Wexler is long gone.

I take each stair carefully and slowly to keep from tripping or making any noise, but by the time I've gone down three floors my footsteps have become the cadence of my fear, racing like my heartbeat. What's wrong with my genome? What will happen if (when) I am caught? What will euthanasia feel like? Will my identicals get any warning, or will someone just round them all up?

My hand clenches around the stair rail with that thought. Other than the carpentry students who saw me marched out of the shed with Trigger, none of my identicals have any idea what I've done.

None of them have ever acted on whatever flaw we share. They don't even know about it. Their ability to efficiently serve the city of Lakeview has not been compromised. So why should they have to pay for my mistake?

I can't run to save my own life and leave them behind to be recalled. But turning myself in won't save my sisters.

Tears blur my vision and I trip over my own foot. I fly forward, grasping for the railing, and my hand catches it at the last second, saving me from a tumble toward the next landing. For a moment, I am paralyzed here in the stairwell, my heart racing even faster than my thoughts, yet I come to that same inevitable conclusion over and over again.

I can't save them. I can't even warn them. Whether or not I escape, they will submit to the recall without ever understanding why they've been sentenced to death.

Poppy will die without ever knowing how badly I betrayed her. How badly I betrayed them all.

My sob echoes through the stairwell. Startled by the sound of my own grief, I slap one hand over my mouth, but I can't hold back the tears. Violet will never take the relay baton from me again, nor smack me with it when she anchors our team victory. Sorrel will never again refuse to trade her tomatoes for my beets by telling me to respect the wisdom of our nutritionists. And Poppy . . .

My eyes fill with tears, blurring the stairs beneath me.

Poppy will never again whisper to me in the dark from her top bunk, fantasizing about the huge gardens we'll oversee after we graduate. Or the two-person bedrooms and lounges rumored to exist in the adult residence halls. Or the grafted plants we'll one day revolutionize hydroponic gardening with.

Every friend I've ever had looks just like me, but we are each different people, and I will miss every one of them in a different way. To a different degree. For a different reason.

I will mourn them as individuals, while the city euthanizes them as one.

Or I will get caught and die with them.

I force myself forward again, and with every step I expect to hear alarms ring out, announcing my escape. They will sound something like the weather siren, I imagine, but I don't know for sure, because I've never heard any other kind. Things like this don't go wrong in Lakeview.

Somehow I am the only thing that has *ever* gone wrong in Lakeview in my lifetime.

After another half a flight, metal squeals over my head as a door opens on the top floor. Panicked, I pull open the door on the sixth-floor landing. A quick glance reveals the end of another empty hallway, so I step into it and pull the door closed as softly as I can.

The soldiers who've come after me don't hear the door, because they're talking. Heart pounding, I face the open end of the sixth-floor hallway so I can see if anyone approaches, then press my ear against the door I've just come through. I'm not sure I'll be able to hear anything over my rushing pulse, yet soon I hear footsteps. Then the soldiers' voices.

I press my cheek harder against the door, the metal cold against my skin, and strain to make out what they're saying.

"Why can't we just raise the alarm and get the whole city looking for her?" the first voice, a woman's, asks.

"Because a recall of five thousand identicals takes some time to set up, and we're not prepared for the panic that would ensue in Workforce if they found out about it before Management had an opportunity to release an official statement," a second female voice replies as their steps clomp closer to the sixth-floor landing. "That, and Ford 45 doesn't want anyone to know he lost not one but two prisoners in a five-minute span until he can also report that they've been recaptured. But even that probably won't save his job."

I exhale slowly. There will be no alarm, and my fellow identicals aren't yet being rounded up. Which means that the best place for me to hide, at least for the moment, is among the 4,999 other girls who look just like me. Without the name embroidered on my athletic jacket, no one will be able to tell me apart from my friends.

When the footsteps and voices have faded, I take off my jacket and stuff it into a trash can halfway down the hall.

Once I am sure the soldiers have had time to reach the bottom floor, I carefully ease the door open again and listen closely. I hear only silence, so I sneak into the stairwell again and continue my quiet descent.

The soldiers' words play over and over in my head. *Recall. Panic.*

How will Lakeview weather the loss of five thousand of its upcoming trade laborers? Aren't we all needed? Who will our teachers teach? Who will our dorm supervisors supervise?

Will it hurt when we die?

My feet pause on the steps when the devastating reality finally hits me. My escape is a far-fetched dream. I still have nowhere to go. I've never even been beyond Lakeview's city walls.

I can't reasonably expect to avoid my fate. But before I die, I *have* to know what Wexler 42 knows.

In what way are we defective?

And if he knew about that defect from the beginning, why was my genome put into production in the first place?

NINE

I huddle in the shadow of the mirrored Management Bureau, staring out at a neatly manicured lawn divided by gently curving sidewalks. As anxious as I am to be moving, I'm terrified to take that first step. On my own I feel unsettlingly conspicuous and vulnerable.

Even without my name embroidered over my heart, I can't simply stroll across the city, much less through the gate into the training ward. The soldiers are looking for a solitary girl who looks just like me. I need camouflage.

My thoughts racing, I glance at the clock tower in the square at the center of the administration ward. Less than an hour has passed since Trigger and I were apprehended. The gardening unions—both landscape and hydroponic—will be back in class already, but because it's field day, several of the other unions should still be in the middle of their exercise unit. Once I make it back to the training ward, all I'll have to do is find another class of my own identicals and blend in until they return to the dormitory to shower.

Getting out of the administration ward will be the real challenge.

I scan the square, and frustration amplifies my fear. Other than soldiers on patrol and the occasional pair of managers headed to or from their bureau, the square is deserted. Is it always like this?

The training ward is always bustling with students. Why are there so few adults out and about in the rest of the city?

Panic closes in on me as I peer out over the nearly empty lawn. Then the familiar rhythm of pounding feet catches my attention. I peek around the corner of the building to see a long cluster of Workforce students jogging along the sidewalk toward the Management Bureau. They're boys—completely useless to me. But behind the boys' class is a girls' class, and behind them is an evidently endless line of jogging students.

And finally I realize what I'm seeing. These are the unions that came in last place during their field day. Rather than victory cupcakes, they get a team-building jog around the training and administrative wards, and their misfortune is my saving grace.

One of these unions is made up of my identicals. And I'm still wearing my athletic uniform.

I watch from my hiding spot as class after class pass me, huffing with exertion. Sixteen year-twelve boys with pale hair and dark eyes. Sixteen year-fourteen girls with red curls and freckles. Sixteen year-seventeen boys with light brown skin and bright greenish eyes. Sixteen year-sixteen girls with . . . my very own face.

My heart beats so hard it hurts.

Because the late fall day has grown warm, my identicals are not wearing their jackets, and with any luck no one will notice one extra.

I steel my nerve and run in place in the shadows until my heart races not from fear but from exertion. Until sweat forms on my forehead. Then, when they pass my hiding place, I slip into their ranks near the end.

As we round the end of the square, I scan the administration grounds and I notice that there are more soldiers out than there were even minutes ago, patrolling in pairs. They're looking for me, yet none of them look *at* me. Alone, identicals stand out, but together, we are never truly seen.

I've never been more grateful for that fact in my life.

I hold my breath as we approach the gate into the training ward, but the guard just waves us through. There are too many of us to bother scanning.

Halfway across the common lawn, the instructor—not one of Belay 35's identicals—calls for a rest. My heart slams against my sternum as the class around me breaks into small groups, talking and drinking from bottles of water.

I don't have a bottle. I have no one to talk to. If I join a group, will they be able to tell I don't belong?

Would I be able to identify an identical stranger among my own classmates?

I would definitely know if anyone tried to impersonate Poppy, Violet, or Sorrel. And I would suspect something if Calla 16 were suddenly friendly. But the rest?

We have assigned desks, gardening stations, and dorm rooms. We tend to sit with the same friends every day in the cafeteria. How much of recognizing my identicals is actually just knowing where they'll be at any given time?

"Blanch, what do you think that's about?" a girl to my left asks.

Blanch. This is a cooking union. The girls around me will have names like Julienne, Simmer, and Braise.

I turn to follow Blanch's gaze and nearly choke on my own tongue. Two identical soldiers are talking to the athletic instructor, gesturing toward the other end of the training ward. Toward the dormitory.

"I don't know," the girl next to Blanch says.

My heart thumping painfully, I casually move closer to the instructor, stopping every few steps to stretch. When I'm a few feet away, I bend to touch my toes and rise with an unattended water bottle.

". . . a security issue. Nothing to worry about," one of the soldiers is saying. But of course it's something to worry about. Defense doesn't dictate the Workforce Academy's schedules.

The instructor frowns. "I don't understand. We still have two laps of the ward before—"

"You'll have to cut the exercise short today," the second soldier interrupts. "We've been instructed to escort your class back to the dormitory, where you're to lead them to their cafeteria for a snack. Management's orders."

"A snack? But they—"

"*Now*, please," the first soldier orders.

The instructor nods stiffly. "Thank you for your service." Then he turns to the rest of us. "Class, we're going to cut the run short." Can the others hear how nervous he sounds? "It seems that Management has an impromptu treat for you in the cafeteria. Please grab your water bottles and follow me."

The girls around me murmur excitedly as we fall into a rough line, and I pass right by the poor girl stuck looking for her missing water bottle.

In the dormitory, when everyone else gathers in front of the bank of elevators, I slip into the stairwell. By the time I reach the eighteenth floor, I'm breathing hard and my quads are on fire. But there is no one on our level to see me sneak from the stairwell into the room I share with Violet, Sorrel, and Poppy. Presumably my union is in class at the academy.

I feel sick thinking about how worried Poppy must be about me.

What has Sorrel 32 told her? What has Sorrel 32 *been told*?

My chest feels like it's caving in. How much time do they have before the recall?

Alone in my dorm room, I feel so jittery that I nearly jump out of my shoes when the air-conditioning suddenly blows my hair from the vent overhead. I strip out of my recreation uniform and toss it down the laundry chute. Since I'm on camera and someone could be watching, I can't spare the time for a shower, so I just change into a clean school uniform. But instead of my own jacket, I take Violet's spare. Her jacket won't fool a scanner held over my wrist, but hopefully wearing her name will prevent my wrist from being scanned in the first place.

Dressed, I glance from bunk to bunk and drawer to drawer. I have no idea what my life will be like from now on, even if I manage to escape the recall. I can't imagine an existence with no identicals. No hydroponics. No classrooms, cafeterias, or group recreation. I can't believe I'm never going to sleep in this room again. I can't believe I'm never going to see my roommates again.

I can't believe my moment of weakness in the equipment shed has led to the imminent euthanasia of five thousand girls. Of every friend I've ever had.

I'm supposed to believe that's inevitable. If a genome is flawed, that flaw will eventually show itself, allowing Lakeview to purge the inferior workers for the benefit of those who remain. Yet that doesn't feel like the case.

Yes, I am attracted to Trigger 17, though doubtless I should not be. But if the elevator hadn't broken down, that attraction would never have had a chance to develop. I would have continued with my life and my work, unaware that such a possibility existed.

Because the flaw in my genome has nothing to do with my ability to grow high-quality crops for the glory of the city.

Or does it?

Even knowing that my life is in danger—that the lives of everyone I've ever known and cared about are in danger—I can't help wondering where Trigger is and hoping he's okay. He's been a distraction from my work and studies for weeks.

Maybe Management is right. Maybe this oddly archaic, strangely physical attraction *does* lead to inefficiency. Maybe my defect *is* relevant to my potential as a gardener.

Has Trigger 17's blood been drawn? Or is such shocking behavior actually acceptable from soldiers expected to react to survival situations with instincts that might save lives?

Maybe his crime isn't *that* he kissed, but *who* he kissed. . . . Maybe his genome will survive this.

Mine will not.

Tears blur my vision and I swipe them from my eyes. I haven't cried since the day I sprained my ankle during a soccer game when I was Dahlia 10.

I don't understand these tears. I'm not injured. Yet I *am* in pain. I ache deep inside but in no location I can describe or point to. Much like I felt when I thought Trigger had graduated.

For the hundredth time, I wish I could warn my sisters, but that would change nothing. Thousands of identicals cannot run, and they cannot hide.

Blinking away more tears, I glance around the room. There's nowhere for me to hide in Lakeview. My only hope of survival is to escape the city. I'm not naive enough to believe that surviving off plants growing in the dirt will be an adventure, but I am confident I can do that. Surely gardeners are uniquely suited to find and identify food growing wild.

I'll need supplies, but if I carry anything obvious I will stand out. So I stuff Violet's jacket pockets with an extra pair of socks and my toothbrush, then I reach for the doorknob. And that's when I realize I have no idea how to get out of the city. There are walls, but I've never been past them. There are gates, but I don't know how to get through them or how long that will take. I've never been farther than the administrative ward. I'm supposed to graduate and be assigned to housing in the residential ward and a job in the industrial ward, where most of the city's hydroponic gardens are located. And it has never occurred to me until *just now* that I might ever need to know any more than that.

I have no idea what to do or where to go. But Trigger goes on missions in the wild. He'll know how to get out of the city. He might even know how to *sneak* out of the city.

He wasn't taken to the Management Bureau with me. If he received some kind of punishment within his own bureau, he'll probably be scrubbing toilets and washing dishes. On the twelfth floor.

TEN

I race down six flights and stand on the twelfth-floor stair-well landing, panting. What if he's not here? Or worse, what if the twelfth floor is crawling with cadets, all aware of my escape and on the lookout for me because they're soldiers in training?

I press my ear to the door, but I can't hear anything, so I take a deep breath and ease it open.

The hallway is deserted. I sneak into it and stand beneath the security camera so it can't see me. A reexamination of the footage will show exactly where I went, but staying out of sight as much as possible on the live feed should buy me some time.

I scoot down the hall with my back pressed against the wall, on alert for the sound of a toilet being scrubbed by a rule-breaking cadet while I assess the threat of each camera

I pass and listen for footsteps. I see and hear nothing but my own thundering heartbeat. If Trigger is being punished in the Defense Academy rather than the dormitory, my escape is doomed.

Near an intersection of the hall, I hear a splash, accompanied by a sigh. I recognize the splat of a mop hitting the floor, and frustration feeds my fear. The custodian trainees may not know that I'm wanted, but they will know I don't belong on the cadets' floor.

Carefully I peek around the corner, expecting to see a member of the manual labor division—the other half of Workforce—hard at work. Instead, I find a cadet with skin a few shades darker than mine and familiar short loose curls slinging a mop back and forth over the already spotless tile floor. His gaze is focused on the tile, his shoulders stiff. He hates this work.

It's Trigger. His shoulder braid is missing—our violation obviously cost him his leadership position—but who else would be mopping tiles as punishment on his dormitory floor?

His mop pauses and he pushes his sleeves up to reach into the wheeled bucket full of murky water. Alarm shoots through my chest, and I scramble silently back from the corner. There's no scar on his arm.

It's not Trigger.

What am I *doing*? My heart slams against my sternum and I close my eyes, fighting for calm. What made me think I could sneak onto a Defense dormitory floor, without getting caught, and find a Special Forces cadet who might not even be there?

I'm a *gardener*.

But if I don't find Trigger and get out of the city, I'm not going to be anything more than a memory—Lakeview's greatest disgrace.

Determined, I peek carefully around the corner again, and when the cadet turns to mop in the other direction I cross the hallway and press my back against the wall on the other side, directly beneath one of the cameras. Quietly I ease my way down this new section of hallway until a deep voice freezes me where I stand.

". . . ever disgrace the unit like that again, Trigger 17, I will see to it that you spend the rest of your life scrubbing toilets and polishing boots." The voice is deep and mature—an instructor or a dormitory conservator. It's coming from an open door two rooms down. "Do you understand, cadet?"

"Yes, Commander."

I exhale, thankful to hear that Trigger is still alive and well. But my relief is fleeting. He's with his commander. Which is surely some kind of instructor. "My biggest regret is that I've embarrassed my unit," Trigger continues.

Embarrassed? Not condemned? Not even shamed?

I've suspected that our infraction wouldn't be as devastating for Trigger as for me and my identicals. I understand that his genome was designed for creative thinking and that subterfuge is part of his training—though I shouldn't understand any of that. But how could the violation that will result in the euthanasia of my entire genome be nothing more than an embarrassment for Trigger and his?

"See that it doesn't happen again," the commander says.

"Yes, sir!" Trigger shouts, even though he's inside, presumably in a small room.

"Dismissed," his commander barks.

Trigger moves into the hall, but his steps falter in front of the doorway when he sees me. I can only stare, panic-stricken. I've found him, and that's as far as my desperate, impulsive plan goes.

The commander's shadow appears in the doorway, but Trigger is still blocking the threshold. Staring at me. "Step aside, cadet."

My heart hammers so loudly it seems to be beating in my head. I need to *move*. But I have no idea where to go.

Trigger's eyes widen, sending me a silent warning I don't know how to heed.

"Now, cadet!" the commander shouts.

Trigger takes one large step out of the door way, opposite the direction I'm standing.

His commander steps into the hall, carrying a tablet, and starts to turn toward me.

My pulse spikes. My hands begin to shake.

"Armstrong 38!" Trigger shouts.

The commander pivots sharply toward him and away from me. "What is it, cadet?" he snaps while I glance around the hall, desperate for some place to hide. If I turn the corner again, the cadet mopping the floor will see me.

"Sir, I respectfully request that you consider returning my braid."

"On what grounds?" Commander Armstrong tucks his arms behind his back, still holding his tablet. The screen shows a large image of my face above print too small for me to read.

He's gotten the alert.

I suck in a quiet, terrified breath and back silently away from them.

"On the grounds that breaking one of the city's most consequential directives took an inordinate amount of courage and ingenuity—two qualities highly valued by Defense leadership."

"Management has been *very clear* about the leniencies afforded cadets in consideration of your training. Defense projects and exercises *may not* affect students from other bureaus. *No exceptions.*"

"And if I'd followed that rule, Management would still be ignorant of a flawed genome less than two years from joining Workforce," Trigger insists. "Lakeview should be thanking me. Instead you're taking my braid."

I stare at him in shocked silence. Is he actually demanding a *reward* for getting me and thousands of my identicals sentenced to death?

It's just a distraction. I can see that. But the fact that his commander is considering his argument tells me more than I want to know about the Defense Bureau.

"Denied." Armstrong 38 starts to turn, and I freeze again.

"On what grounds?" Trigger demands, and I flinch. I've never heard anyone speak to an instructor like this.

The commander spins toward Trigger, clutching his tablet so tightly that his fingers have gone white. "On the grounds that you got caught, cadet. Special Forces *does not get caught*."

I glance around the hallway again, my heart racing. Halfway down, a plaque marks one closed door as a supply closet. The doorknob has no keyhole. It can't be locked.

"Respectfully, sir, if I hadn't gotten caught, my actions would have gone unnoticed. And unrewarded," Trigger adds as I creep softly toward the closet.

"Are you saying you got caught on purpose? Cadet, did it ever occur to you to simply make a report?" Armstrong 38 demands. "You would have gotten credit for what you uncovered, but you *would not have been caught*."

Surprise washes over Trigger's strong features as I ease open the closet door, crossing my fingers that the hinges don't squeak. "In retrospect, that does seem to be the wisest course of action," he admits.

"Indeed," Armstrong 38 grunts. "This is your last warning. If I hear your name again before graduation, I'll have you bumped down to infantry."

"Sir, you can't—!"

"You are out of line!" Commander Armstrong shouts as I close the closet door.

"Yes, sir." Trigger's voice is softer, heard through the door, but he sounds relieved. I am hidden. He can stop arguing with his commander. "I apologize, sir."

The only reply is Armstrong's swift, heavy footsteps marching past my hiding place, headed toward the bank of elevators.

When I hear the doors slide closed, I exhale. A second later, the storage closet door flies open, and before I can gasp Trigger tugs me into the hall by one hand.

"Slide along the wall, beneath the camera," he whispers, obviously unaware that I've already figured that out.

We make our way quickly down the hall, my hand still clasped in his, and even though my need to flee the city grows more urgent with every passing second, the feeling of his palm pressed against mine is strangely reassuring. And exhilarating.

Trigger sticks his wrist beneath the scanner next to a door halfway down, and a green light flashes as the bolt slides back.

"Step to the right and stay against the wall," he whispers as he opens the door.

I follow his instructions and find a dorm room strikingly similar to mine. Two sets of neatly made bunk beds. Drawers and chutes built into the wall. But there is no rug. There are no chairs. There are no sketches of plants hung on the walls.

Nothing differentiates one bunk from the next.

Trigger leaves the door open at a precise and odd angle. Puzzled, I follow his gaze and see that at this angle, the open door blocks me and half of the room from the camera's view.

"In there," he whispers, and I hurry silently into the bathroom, careful to keep my back against the wall. Inside I exhale slowly. It would never have occurred to me to hide from the cameras using an open door, but Trigger 17 is obviously accustomed to evading observation.

What did he use these skills for before he met me?

He steps into the bathroom and closes the door, and his soft frown is equal parts relieved and concerned. And a little impressed. "How did you get in here? How did you get out of *custody?*"

"I had help with a door lock. Then I snuck out and jogged across the city with a class of cooks."

Trigger looks at me as if he's seeing me for the first time. "Are you sure you're a gardener? Because that sounds more like something a cadet would do in training."

"They teach you how to escape?"

He nods. "From a variety of situations. In case we're ever captured." He takes a deep breath and lets it out slowly.

"Did you mean any of what you said to that Commander? Would you have turned me in for a greater leadership position, if you'd thought of it?"

"I *did* think of it. The day we got stuck in the elevator. Back before I'd committed any infraction. But I couldn't do it."

"*What?* You spoke to me first!"

"Yes, but only in an official capacity." He smiles, and this time when my gaze catches on his mouth, all I want to do is punch it. "You were going to hyperventilate, and I'm trained to prevent that. What was I supposed to do? Let you pass out? Defense would have considered that a humanitarian effort, not a violation."

"You mean I was the *only one* breaking a rule in that elevator?"

"Yes. But I've broken plenty since then. Dahlia, I could never have turned you in." His smile fades as he looks into my eyes. "I was afraid they'd recall your genome."

"They did. They are, I mean." My throat tries to close around the words. "Evidently coordinating a recall that large takes time."

"I'm so sorry. I didn't mean for any of this to happen." His voice sounds strained. As if he's in physical pain. "I followed you into the equipment shed thinking we could steal a few minutes, but Mace 17 saw. He wanted my red braid. So he turned me in."

"He did this for a braid?" The petty nature of such an act stuns me. "He must have known what would happen to my genome. He would do that for an *accessory?*"

"For what the braid represents. For the respect and benefits that come with a leadership position. But they won't give it to him. Locking your roommate in a closet when you're a year seven is one thing. Betraying him to the enemy—to Management, in this case—when you're months from graduating is something else entirely. At this point in our training, we're supposed to be able to trust one another implicitly."

"So he doomed Poppy and all the rest of my identicals for nothing?" Though it hardly seems possible, that makes me feel even worse.

"I'm so sorry." Trigger's gaze strays to my lips, and I feel a ghost of our kiss haunting me with its consequences. "I wanted to bring you something picked fresh from the wild. I wanted to touch you again," he says. "I saw you and I couldn't resist."

I understand that feeling. That horrific, exhilarating certainty that you're going to touch something dangerous—something that *will* hurt you—because you *have* to know what it feels like. Just this once.

He frowns. "I should have known better. I should have been more careful."

Yes. And so should I.

Trigger reaches for my hand in spite of the conclusion we've both drawn, and I let him have it, because I am already in as much danger as I can possibly get into. He's the reason my whole world is falling apart, yet somehow being near him is comforting when it should be terrifying.

"It doesn't matter," I tell him as the inevitability of my predicament settles onto my shoulders like a weight pressing me into the ground. "If Management is right, my flawed genome would have showed itself eventually."

"There's nothing wrong with you, unless the same thing's wrong with me." Trigger leans down to kiss me, but I push him away, even though every flawed cell in my body aches to pull him closer. I can't kiss him knowing that Management is planning the systematic destruction of nearly everyone I've ever known. Kissing Trigger got my entire genome recalled.

No, Mace 17 got my genome recalled. Genetic flaws got my genome recalled.

I got my genome recalled.

But I'm going to die if Management catches me, and if I escape the city I'll never see Trigger again. These are the last moments we'll ever spend together.

So I pull him closer and step up on my toes. His hands find my waist, and my arms wrap around his neck. I kiss him, and this kiss is deeper and wilder. Desperate and scared. I can feel time slipping away from us, and no matter how tightly I hold him, soon I'll have to let go.

When I finally pull away, my pulse racing, I'm hyperaware of how long I've spent in Trigger's room. Yet I don't regret a single second of that kiss.

"I have to go." Reluctantly I let my arms slide free of his neck. "Can you tell me how to get out of the city? I . . ." My ignorance is humiliating. "I don't even know where the gate is."

Trigger's grip on me tightens. "There are several gates, Dahlia, but you can't go through any of them. Your bar code won't open them, and most of them are guarded. You'll be arrested the moment they see you."

"Only *most* of them are guarded? What about the unguarded gates?"

He lets me go. "Neither of us has the security clearance to unlock them, and if we try we'll be raising an alarm." He holds his arm up, showing me the bar code on his wrist for emphasis.

"Trigger, there has to be a way out."

"Not on your own. But I can help." He squats in front of the cabinet below his sink and pulls out a small zippered bag.

"No." I shake my head firmly. "I'm not going to drag

you—" I frown as he opens the medicine cabinet and pulls out a half-empty tube of toothpaste. "What are you doing?"

"Packing. I'm in trouble whether I go with you or not, but you won't make it out of the city without my help. So I'm coming with you."

I should tell him no again, but I'm not ready to say good-bye. I want to know what life is like as a cadet. I want to know what he thinks about at night before he falls asleep. I want to know what he likes to eat and how he got the tiny scar on his thumb.

I want to know what these feelings mean.

Would I have this same attraction for any boy I got stuck in an elevator with, or is this attraction specific to Trigger 17? He must have felt this before. How else would he have known about kissing? How does his attraction to me compare to what he's felt for girls in the past? Am I the only girl outside of his union he's had a conversation with?

I will never have those answers if he doesn't come with me.

I will never get to kiss him again if he stays behind.

"Okay. Come with me."

He smiles, but I know I've made the wrong decision as soon as the words fall from my lips. I am damning him to my fate. I might also be damning his entire genome. "Wait. Will your identicals suffer for this?"

"No," he insists as he drops a toothbrush into the bag. "I was trained to follow orders, but I was designed to think for myself."

"Those seem like two conflicting concepts."

"Sometimes it feels that way." Trigger takes the third of four razors lined up on the counter and drops it into the bag. "Following orders is always our primary objective, but out in the field the method isn't as important as the result. My genome is intentionally inventive and bold to help us survive on missions and in the wild. And those who think as individuals are treated as individuals."

"So what will they think when you're just . . . gone?"

"Management will tell the cadets I died in the wild on some kind of test or mission."

"But that's a *lie!*"

"Management doesn't lie." Trigger stands up straight and gives me a look that makes me feel very young. Very inexperienced. "Neither does Defense. They simply make strategic omissions, as authorized by the city's official security bylaws. Anything necessary to protect the city is permissible. To keep everyone safe and productive."

Safe and productive. Those words are printed on Lakeview's official seal, displayed on the side of every CitiCar and on the floor of the Management Bureau's lobby. Everything Management does is to keep the city safe and productive— including the rare recall of flawed genomes.

The recall is a normal, necessary process. Even in the wild, flawed plants and animals die. Right?

Yet again, I find myself inexplicably unwilling to die, despite the selfishness inherent in that thought. I'm not done living. I'm not done knowing, finding, feeling, seeing, and touching. I'm not done *being*.

I wish my identicals weren't done either. I wish I knew how to help them.

Trigger zips up his toiletry bag. "We should go." He opens the bathroom door to another very specific angle, then motions for me to make my way along the wall again. While I sneak toward the door, he glances around his dorm room from the middle of the floor, his brows drawn into a straight, determined line. "We'll need more supplies." He opens a closet door and lifts a worn olive-green backpack from the floor.

"Won't we stand out if we carry a bag?"

Trigger shrugs as he shoves things into the pack from his bureau drawer. "If we're seen together, we'll stand out. I don't think a backpack could make that much worse."

I'm fascinated to realize that his entire life will fit into that one bag.

Mine would probably take up even less space.

"What are those?" I ask from my position beneath the camera as he tosses in a small cardboard box.

"Matches. It'll get cold at night, and we'll need fire to cook meat."

I was taught the theoretical basics of cooking as it applies to my job, but I've never seen a match. I've never felt the warmth of an open flame. Those things have no relevance to the life of a hydroponic gardener.

With a disquieting bolt of surprise, I realize I am no longer a gardener. I will probably never pick up another pH tester or fill another water pan.

If I was designed for trade labor and trained as a hydroponic gardener yet can never be either of those again, what am I now?

Who am I?

ELEVEN

Trigger shows me the pattern of steps and pauses needed to sneak past the cameras on his floor. I'm sure at least three of them caught glimpses of me—and probably of him—but if no one is watching the feeds live, our escape from the dormitory won't be discovered until someone realizes he's missing and examines the footage.

We hope to be long gone by then.

We are twenty feet from the stairwell when a familiar voice freezes me in place, my left shoulder inches from a glass window set into the stark white wall where the conservator's office is on my floor.

". . . wanted to personally thank you, Commander Armstrong, for volunteering two of your field medic classes to oversee the blood tests."

It's Ford 45. I'm *certain* it's him. If I got any closer to the window, I could peek in and tell for sure. But that would be too much of a risk.

"The assistance has truly helped us speed the process along," Ford continues. "Five thousand tests in two hours is quite a challenge."

"We were happy to help increase your efficiency. Is the task well under way?"

"It's just now completed," Ford answers. "We only have preliminary results so far, but they are unprecedented. Dahlia 16's genetic examination revealed two specific and very odd flaws, yet not one of her identicals has tested positive for either of them so far."

The cadet instructor's gasp drowns out my own. "How is that possible?"

"We don't know yet. But we will get to the bottom of this."

Trigger squats and tugs on my hand, trying to get me to crawl past the window, but I'm stuck in place, both horrified for what this revelation might mean for me and relieved for my identicals.

If they're not flawed, they won't have to be recalled. Right?

"How will you proceed with the identicals?" Armstrong 38 asks.

"We will carry on with the recall to maintain public confidence in Management, and in our geneticists, and in the entire system."

What? My stomach begins to churn. I sink to the floor next to Trigger, and the tile feels cold against my knees through the stretchy material of my athletic pants.

"That is wise," the commander replies. "Faith in the system is ultimately of far more importance than any individual within it."

What about five thousand *individuals?*

They're still talking, but I'm lost in my own head. In the senselessness of the loss. If none of my sisters are flawed, why recall them?

Trigger pulls on my hand again, and again I refuse to move. I have to know what's wrong with me. Why my defects will mean doom for thousands of perfectly perfect girls.

"But there's something else you could help me with, Commander," Ford says. "This boy she was caught with. This cadet . . ." During the pause, I picture him consulting a tablet. "Trigger 17."

Trigger stops tugging me.

"It turns out they got stuck in an elevator together a few weeks ago, and we think that was the beginning of this whole mess. Nearly an hour with no power or camera."

Armstrong 38 grunts. "Yes, I remember his report, but he didn't mention there was another student with him."

I glance at Trigger and find his jaw tense.

"Interesting." Ford clears his throat. "What kind of boy is he?"

Trigger tries to pull me forward again, but I tug free of his grip. I want to hear this too.

"He's a capable student and an excellent fighter. They all are. However, Trigger 17 is *particularly* creative and determined. Until today he was a squad leader and a very strong candidate for leadership within the Defense—"

"Yes, I've seen his record. But what kind of *boy* is he?" Ford asks. "How is he . . . socially? You heard how they were caught?"

Trigger scowls as he tries to pull me forward, but I am caught in this discussion like a fly in a web.

"Oh." Armstrong clears his throat. "Most cadets are *social*. It's a result of the otherwise vestigial hormones necessary to grow a fighter, both physically and mentally. You can't get the increased bone density, musculature, and interest in the subject matter without also tapping into another kind of primal instinct."

"I see," Ford 45 says. "Your explanation is much simpler and less technical than that of the geneticist I just spoke to."

Armstrong laughs. "It's harmless. We allow the male and female units to fraternize in their free time. That lets them get it out of their systems so they can concentrate during class and training."

Trigger tugs on my hand again, more urgently this time, and I notice that his face is flushed. Is he . . . embarrassed? Or angry?

I feel like he understands more of what we're hearing than I do.

Reluctantly I begin to crawl slowly past the window.

"But she's not Defense," Armstrong adds. "Trigger's influence on her will have been minimal."

"Because the other bureaus aren't saddled with the distraction of primitive hormones?"

"Exactly. She shouldn't have much interest in him beyond idle curiosity."

The commander is wrong.

Why is he so *very* wrong?

"I'd like to speak with this cadet, if I may." Yet Ford 45 seems to be giving an order rather than making a request.

"Of course. I'll call him in—"

"After the recall. We're going to need the rest of your cadets a little longer," Ford 45 says as I listen from beneath the window. "If you're amenable, of course."

"To help with the recall?"

"No, Management can handle that. But what's left of your year seventeens will give us the manpower to double up on patrols in the training ward. Dahlia 16 has been officially labeled an anomaly, and between the two of us . . . she's unaccounted for."

"She *escaped*? That *does* sound anomalous for a trade laborer."

Trigger grins at the surprise in his commander's voice, as if I should be proud of what I've done. Of surviving this far. But I feel only guilt for the fate of my identicals.

The word *anomaly* rolls around in my head. I'm familiar with the concept as it refers to plants. To irregularities, which typically result in the destruction of the affected specimen. But I've never heard of an anomalous *person*.

Yet I'd never heard of a beautiful person either until Trigger introduced me to that concept, so maybe people can be anomalous too. Maybe people, like plants, sometimes inexplicably defy the cloning process that is supposed to render them genetically flawless and indistinguishable from their identicals. The process that is supposed to give them the comfort and security of familiar faces and a place to belong.

But when an anomalous plant blooms in class, we only destroy that one specimen. We don't trash the entire crop yield! Euthanizing 4,999 flawless girls would be unbelievably wasteful and inefficient. Contrary to the very ideals Lakeview holds in esteem.

What could Management possibly be thinking?

Trigger's grip on my hand tightens. His lips form my name silently as he begs me to come with him before we're discovered.

"And our orders?" Commander Armstrong says, recapturing my attention. "Are you authorizing lethal force?"

My heart leaps into my throat and sticks there. What does that mean? They want Trigger's identicals to *shoot* me?

"No!" Ford 45 sounds almost as horrified as I feel. "Dahlia 16 must be brought in alive for a thorough examination."

Examination? Somehow that sounds much less agreeable than my yearly physical.

"We need to know how this happened so we can prevent future such disasters in the genetics lab," Ford continues.

"Your boys and girls are on a find-and-report mission only. Without a union to blend into, Dahlia 16 should be easy to find."

Nausea washes over me. Is that why my defectless sisters are being recalled? To make it easier for Management and Defense to hunt me?

I follow Trigger toward the staircase. I've already heard too much, and I can't process all the information clunking around in my head. Each bit feels like a jigsaw puzzle piece that doesn't match the image on the box. The image of a city I thought I knew. A life I thought I understood.

We crawl several feet past the window before we stand, just in case, but then we race silently toward the end of the hall, heedless of the cameras.

Trigger opens the stairwell door slowly to keep it from squealing. I step inside and he uses his free hand to close the heavy door as slowly as he opened it. I can no longer hear Ford 45 and the commander talking, yet I can't unhear what they've already said.

Anomaly.

Recall.

Examination.

Trigger takes the first three steps quickly and silently in his boots, and there's years of training in each graceful motion.

I have no training. So far I've survived on luck. But that will have to change.

I take that first step, but I can't feel the tread beneath my foot. I can't feel the sweat that has gathered behind my knees and between my breasts. I can't feel the air I inhale as I stare at our intertwined fingers.

"Dahlia, we have to go."

I take another step, then another, and soon we're flying down the stairs together, and it feels a bit like talking to him in the Workforce Bureau stairwell, only more dangerous and terrifying and somehow exhilarating. Because this time I'm not just supposed to be somewhere else.

I'm supposed to be dead.

After they finish examining me, Management will complete their recall and I will become the five thousandth brown-eyed, brown-haired, right-handed sixteen-year-old female corpse.

Trigger seems even more determined than I am not to let that happen to me.

But I can't let that happen to *anyone*. I can't let Poppy, or Sorrel, or Violet be . . .

How would they die? Gas, or injection, or one of the other supposedly humane ways governments put people to death in our barbaric past?

I stop several steps above the fourth-floor landing, and Trigger turns to look up at me. "We have to help them." I'm breathless, not from the exertion, but from the horror of what's about to happen if we can't stop it.

"Help who?"

My best friend. My roommates.

"The four thousand nine hundred ninety-nine girls who

look just like me, Trigger. Gardeners, electricians, plumbers, medical technicians, carpenters, mechanics, and dozens of other trade laborers. They're going to die, even though there's nothing wrong with them, unless we do something!"

He glances down the stairwell, and I can see urgency in the motion. "What can we do? Even if we could free them from wherever they're being held, where would we take them?"

"There has to be somewhere we could hide them. I mean, if you can hack the security cameras and the communication feeds, couldn't you type something somewhere and make it look like they've already been recalled?"

"Probably," Trigger admits, yet his forehead is more furrowed than I've ever seen it. "But I can't hack into people's brains and make them remember doing something they never did. Like euthanizing five thousand identicals."

"We have to try. Wouldn't you try to save your identicals if they were being recalled?"

"My identicals are cadets. We know from the time we can walk that someday we'll die in the service of this city."

"So your friends would just line up to be killed?" That doesn't sound much like the only cadet I've actually met.

Trigger's frown deepens, as if he's considering that question for the first time. "Well, no, if they didn't believe their deaths would benefit the city, they'd probably fight. That's what we're trained to do. But no one in their right mind would tell an entire division of Defense cadets that they're about to be euthanized. They'd have to do it without warning us. Maybe while we were asleep." He shrugs, and I'm pleased to see that he at least looks bothered by the idea. "But your sisters aren't cadets."

"That doesn't mean they won't fight. If they know what's about to happen—if they know that they're not flawed and their existence is no real threat to the city—they'll fight." I grip the stair rail in white-knuckled determination. Poppy loves a good argument. I can't believe she wouldn't fight for her life. And if she would, others might. "Even five thousand untrained girls have a shot at overwhelming whoever's in charge of the recall if those in charge aren't expecting it."

Isn't that possibility exactly why the recall hasn't been announced? To avoid panic that might lead to unrest. Insubordination.

Trigger takes a deep breath and lets it out slowly. "Dahlia, do you understand what you're suggesting?"

"I . . ." I'm suggesting the only thing I can think of that might actually save every friend I've ever had from pointless euthanasia, but I haven't given much thought to the bigger picture: what that will mean for us afterward.

"You're talking about a rebellion. A revolt, albeit with teenage girls rather than armed militants." Trigger leans against the concrete stairwell wall, crossing his arms over his chest. "The city will never stand for that."

"What do we have to lose? Management is going to kill them all anyway, so if we fight and die we're no worse off than we would be if we didn't fight in the first place."

"No, *they're* no worse off. If we run now, you and I might make it out. If we fight with your sisters, we'll probably all die."

I don't even try to hide my disappointment from him. "I thought you were prepared to die."

"I am. But I'm not prepared to see *you* die."

My chest aches again. There is a strangely raw, vulnerable quality in his voice now that makes my heart feel as if my lungs are suddenly shrinking around it. "I don't want to die either, Trigger, but I'm not sure I can go on living knowing that all my sisters died and I did nothing to try to stop it."

"They're right, Dahlia." His focus on my eyes intensifies, as if he's looking for something. Or maybe he's found something. "You are different from the others."

TWELVE

Trigger stares at me in the dim stairwell, and I can almost see him weighing his options. I'm not leaving Poppy or any of the others here to die.

Finally he nods. "Okay. Let me see what I can find out." He pulls a small tablet from the inside pocket of his uniform jacket and begins to tap and scroll. "You know this is crazy, right?"

I'm not sure I understand. According to my year-twelve social anthropology unit, *crazy* means mentally disordered. The inability to draw or keep one's thoughts in logical order.

Is that one of my defects?

I glance up at Trigger, and with one look at my face he gives me a small smile. "It's an expression. Do they not say that in Workforce?"

I shake my head.

"It means that only someone with an inability to see the logical flaws in our plan would go through with it. But you're not literally insane." Trigger turns back to his tablet. "I can get into your instructor's feed again, but since Sorrel 32 isn't Management, she might not have access to the information we're looking for, and we don't have time for me to hack anyone else's account."

I'm not sure I understand that either, but I nod anyway.

"Okay," he says a few taps later. "It looks like a bulletin went out to all the year-sixteen trade labor division instructors a couple of hours ago. They were asked to bring all their classes to the Defense Bureau in staggered time slots. That's probably where the blood tests were performed. It's probably also where the recall will take place. Rumor has it there's an underground level only the top-ranking Defense officials have access to for that very purpose."

I try to swallow my horror. "There's a secret killing level in the Defense Bureau?"

"Its existence isn't the secret. It's the location most people don't know."

"Can you tell if they're still there?"

"Not from Sorrel 32's feed. Your instructors won't have the security clearance to access the specifics on this. Mine won't either. That'll be limited to top-tier Defense and Management officials."

"Okay. Can you get us into the building?"

Trigger shrugs as he slides his tablet back into an inner

pocket. "Yes, until they discover what I'm doing and strip my access."

Which won't be long, if anyone has discovered him missing. "So we need to go now."

"We need to have gone two hours ago."

My shoes hardly hit the fourth-floor landing before we're past it, only three flights from the ground now. I look up at the spiral of stairs above us and I can't believe how far we've come already. Yet how far we still have to go.

"We can't just march across the city," Trigger says as I try to match each of his silent steps with one of my own. "We need a plan."

"I have one." I stop, panting, at the very bottom of the stairwell with nothing except a single steel door separating me from an entire city that wants me dead. "We're going to march across the city. Or rather, you're going to march *me* across the city. Your whole division's supposed to be looking for me, right? Do you have one of those plastic restraints like they put on us in the equipment shed?"

"You want me to pretend to have caught you?" Trigger looks intrigued.

"That would let you walk us both right up to the building, wouldn't it?"

"They'll take custody of you the second they see you. They'll do that before we get to the bureau, if anyone from Management or Defense sees us on the way."

"So we avoid the common lawns and go behind the

buildings instead. We can sneak most of the way and only walk boldly when there's a chance we'll be seen. Will that work?"

Trigger shrugs. "I doubt it. But your plan's better than anything I've come up with. However, the hard part will be getting past the gate into the administration ward."

"Oh." Of course. "Um . . ."

"There's a gate on the back side of the training ward that only has one guard. It's mostly used for shipping. I think that's our best bet."

"Okay. So the plastic restraint?" I glance at his waist and notice for the first time that he's not wearing an equipment belt like full-fledged soldiers do. "*Please* tell me those are standard-issue?"

"For a cadet? No. But I might know where we can get one." Trigger eases open the interior stairwell door. Over his shoulder I see an empty first-floor hallway. He closes the door softly, then opens the exterior door on the right. Even before I see grass and sky, I hear footsteps and voices. Instinctively I back away, but Trigger doesn't seem worried, and after a second I realize why. The voices and footsteps are heading away from us.

The last place anyone expects a girl on the run to go is back to her dormitory.

I can't decide whether that makes me stupid or brilliant.

Trigger removes his backpack—it would be a dead giveaway in our new plan—and takes my hand again as we step out of the stairwell onto a sidewalk that hugs the side of the dormitory. It's mostly used by the grounds crew and manual labor division, who push carts and wheelbarrows loaded with supplies from the delivery bay at the back of the . . .

The delivery bay.

"No!" I whisper, tugging Trigger to a stop. "We'll be seen."

"No, we won't. Most shipments come in the morning." He pulls on my hand again, and I follow him around the building, hugging the wall with the hope that the afternoon shadows will hide us. "This time of day, the bay should be deserted, except for . . ." Instead of finishing his sentence, he levels an openhanded, triumphant gesture at two vehicles sitting at the curb, straddling the cruise strip.

One car is blue with the Lakeview city seal painted on the side. It's a patrol car.

The other is neither a patrol car nor a CitiCar, open to use by the general public. For adults, anyway. CitiCars are all bright yellow and numbered. This car is shiny and black, and its windows are so tinted I can't see inside. It's a personal vehicle, and those are only issued to very important people.

Bureau chiefs. Management officials. The Administrator. It must belong to Ford 45.

Trigger lets go of my hand. "I'll be right back," he whispers, then jogs across the bay toward the patrol car, hunched over. He pulls open one of the front doors and reaches into the small compartment beneath the dashboard. A second later he is jogging toward me again with not just one but several white plastic restraint strips.

"You sure you want to do this?" he whispers, holding them up for my inspection.

"I'm sure I don't have any other choice." I turn and put my hands behind my back, and even though I've volunteered for this I am almost as scared as I was when the real soldiers restrained me in the equipment shed.

The plastic is cold against my wrists, and I can both hear and feel the zipping sensation when he pulls one end through the slot on the other. He leaves it loose enough to be comfortable. I flex my wrists and realize that if I have to, I can pull myself free.

"Just in case," he explains.

"Does it look too loose?"

"If anyone gets close enough to notice, we'll have bigger problems to worry about. You ready?"

I wouldn't be ready even if I had a decade to prepare. Instead of answering, I turn and hold one bent elbow toward him.

Trigger wraps his hand around my arm and takes a deep breath. I wonder if he can possibly be as nervous about this as I am, but there's no time to ask, because in the next moment we're moving, not toward the common lawn but away from it. Toward the rear of the dormitory and the little-used walkway connecting it to the rear entrances of many other buildings in the training ward.

It's a ten-minute walk from the dorm to the small gate he mentioned, but it feels like forever with my hands restrained at my back. With the possibility of a very real arrest hanging over my head.

Every rustle of tree limbs in the fall breeze makes me flinch. Every bird chirp raises my pulse. And when I hear footsteps headed our way, my feet try to spread roots into the sidewalk beneath me.

Two instructors round the corner of the Specialist Academy, where doctors, dentists, and other highly trained and educated genomes are taught, and their conversation stops when they see us.

Trigger pulls me forward with more force than he would have used if he weren't pretending to have apprehended me, and to my relief the instructors seem to believe our act.

"Did you see the bulletin?" one asks the other.

His friend nods. "The entire year-sixteen trade labor division. They must still be rounding them up."

"Using cadets?"

"Yes. Didn't you get that ping?"

We're too far away by then to catch any more, but I've heard what I needed to. My plan is a good one, and Trigger is playing his part well. Yet every single step is loaded with the terrifying possibility that we will be caught.

We see several more small groups of people on the way. All of them are instructors or supervisors, and though they all stop to watch, none of them question us or seem to doubt that we're anything other than what we appear to be. Possibly because we haven't yet gone far enough to encounter anyone from Defense or Management.

When we reach the rear of the Arts Academy, Trigger pulls me to a stop in the shadow of the building. "There's the gate."

He points and I see that he's right. The gate is open, and there's only one guard.

But one is all it takes to sound an alarm.

I turn back to find Trigger studying the guard, a Defense graduate in his mid-twenties whose gaze constantly scans the training ward grounds.

"We just need a distraction. . . ." Trigger eyes the trees near the gate, then a car approaching along the cruise strip. "Something big enough to get his attention but too small to require backup."

A camera positioned over the gate catches my eye as it rotates, constantly surveying a new slice of the common lawn. Fifty feet away is another camera, around a slight bend and just out of sight of the guard.

"Remember when you said you could hack the cameras?" I whisper. "Can you give us another little malfunction?"

Trigger follows my line of sight and smiles. Then he pulls his tablet from his pocket and starts tapping. A minute later the red light on the far camera goes off.

A second after that, the guard pulls his tablet from his own pocket and frowns. He glances to his left but can't see the camera around the curve.

"There he goes," Trigger whispers when the guard reluctantly leaves his post to check out the malfunctioning camera. "It'll come back on in three minutes. Let's go." When I hesitate, trying to calm the nerves fluttering in my stomach, Trigger leans closer to whisper, "Walk as if you belong and that's what people will believe."

I let him march me toward the gate as quietly and quickly as we dare without attracting even more attention. I can't see anyone watching us, and with any luck, anyone who is will believe our charade.

It's a short walk from the small gate to the back of the Specialist Bureau, and by the time we reach the far corner, clinging to the shadows cast by the building, we can see the Defense Bureau.

"Okay," Trigger whispers. "We need to find a way inside without being seen." He pulls out his tablet again. "If they've figured out I'm missing, then scanning my bar code at any door will raise an alarm. So we really need to . . ."

His voice fades into the background as a loud rumble comes from the opposite side of the Defense Bureau. "What's that?" I whisper. Then I have to repeat my question a little louder so he can hear me.

"Sounds like . . . engines." Trigger looks up from his tablet, frowning as the first vehicle rounds the far side of the Defense Bureau. It follows the cruise strip painted on the road like any normal car, but there is nothing else normal about this vehicle. It's *huge*. At least fifty feet long. It looks kind of like a giant, completely enclosed delivery cart.

At the front is a passenger compartment holding a single man. A soldier.

Behind the first vehicle comes another. Then another. Then another.

"What are those?" I ask.

Trigger doesn't answer until I elbow him and repeat the

143

question. "Cargo trucks. They're used to deliver goods we trade with other cities. But . . ."

"But supplies aren't shipped from the Defense Bureau," I murmur as I watch the procession of trucks. Something isn't right. I can feel that from the goose bumps that have risen on my skin all the way to the strange ache in my bones. "They come from the central warehouse."

"And soldiers don't make deliveries," he adds. "Goods are always delivered by high-ranking members of Management."

The line of trucks stretches farther than we can see from where we're hidden, and there seems to be no end in sight.

"Are soldiers deployed in trucks like that?" I ask, desperate for a logical explanation to calm the unease crawling over me.

"No. Troop transport trucks have removable canvas tops. And I've never seen more than a few of those dispatched at a time. They carry up to eighty bodies each, and this many could carry hundreds. Maybe thousands . . ."

We both seem to hear what he's said at the same time.

Bodies. Thousands.

He meant living bodies, but . . .

"No." I shake my head over and over. I can't stop. Sorrel and Violet, and . . . Poppy.

All those nights we stayed up whispering. All those lunches spent criticizing the mushy veggies on our trays and imagining how *we'd* cook them. A thousand smiles and laughs, and at least a hundred field day victories, when I'd trade my icing for her cake.

She *can't* be gone. I can't even imagine the world without her.

"Hold on. Let me check." Trigger taps on his tablet again while I watch the never-ending procession of cargo trucks with tears in my eyes. "Your instructor doesn't have access to any useful information. I need someone else's account. . . ."

"How do they do it?"

"Hmm?" But he's still tapping and scrolling. "I can't access the camera feed. Someone has locked it down. Wait. I have one feed. It's broadcasting from the loading bay behind the Defense Bureau. There're still a dozen trucks back there." He holds the tablet toward me, but I can't look. I can't turn away from the procession still rolling by. "They're just waiting in line."

"Trigger, how do they *do* it?" I demand softly. "The recall. Did they feel anything?"

"You don't know that they're in those trucks, Dahlia." He's tapping again.

"What else would Lakeview have to deliver by the thousands, from the Defense Bureau with its secret killing level, on the very day my genome is scheduled to be recalled?" Nothing else makes sense.

Not that the truth makes sense either. There was nothing wrong with them. They were no threat to the efficiency of the city or the citizens' faith in Management's ability to lead.

They didn't need to die.

Trigger makes a strange noise deep in his throat, and I

turn away from the parade of trucks to see him staring at his tablet. "A bulletin just went out to all your instructors. It's done. There's a crematorium a few miles outside of the—"

"No." I heard him. I knew the truth even before I heard him. But I can't . . .

I can't . . .

I can't . . .

THIRTEEN

Trigger pulls a small folding knife from his pocket, but I hardly feel it when he cuts the restraint from my wrists. The plastic falls to the ground, and dimly I realize that someone will find it eventually, and they might figure out that we were here. That we saw the caravan. That I was not in one of those trucks.

But they'll never know the full story. Management won't let that happen. They just killed almost five thousand people to prevent that very thing.

"Shh . . . ," Trigger whispers into my ear, his arms around my shoulders, his jaw scruff catching in my hair, and that's when I realize I'm crying. I am bawling and gasping and choking on tears. My nose is running. The entire world looks like a watercolor painting viewed too closely through my tear-filled eyes.

It wasn't supposed to be like this. The recall.

They told us that recalls were good. That they were necessary to preserve order. To keep the rest of us safe and productive.

But that's not what this is. This is pointless death. This is thousands and thousands of lives *stolen*. Our violent, wasteful ancestors had a brutal, ugly name for this.

Murder.

Lakeview just *murdered* my best friend. *All* my friends. Nearly everyone I've ever known. Management thought that if they recalled an entire genome, there would be no one left to miss the missing. But *I'm* left. *I* miss them.

"Just hold it together long enough for me to find someplace safe," Trigger whispers.

But there is no place safe. That's the whole problem.

Trigger turns away from me, and I hear the scrape of metal against metal. His knife is out again. He's forcing a lock. A second later he pulls open a heavy door and tugs me into a narrow space with a big echo. Another stairwell.

"Where are we?" I sob, wiping my eyes, but the effort is futile. The tears won't stop.

"The Specialist Bureau. The workday is over. There won't be anyone here but the night cleaning crew, and if we stay in the stairwell we won't have to worry about cameras. But I need you to get it together. We can't stay here long. The longer they go without catching you, the wider and more thorough the search will be."

Get it together. That sounds like nonsense.

How am I supposed to get myself together when we just saw several dozen truckloads of bodies roll toward the city gate? When almost everyone I've ever known in my entire life is dead? Because of me.

There is no getting it together.

In the back of my mind, in spite of everything that had gone wrong, I believed there was a way to fix this. We could tell everyone that my identicals weren't flawed. We could fight. We could escape into the wild together and Poppy, Trigger, and I could make some kind of "crazy," primitive life on our own. Harvesting wild vegetables. Hunting wild . . . cows. Or whatever soldiers learn to hunt and cook.

But that was never anything more than a fantasy, and now that fantasy is as dead as every friend I've ever had.

I will never see another face that looks just like mine.

Nothing will ever be okay again.

Trigger opens each door a crack, one at a time, to make sure no one's approaching from the first floor of the Specialist Bureau or from outside. Then he pulls me into a hug. But that only makes me cry harder.

I cling to him. I don't know how to stop, and he doesn't seem to care that I'm getting tears and snot on the shoulder of his uniform jacket.

"Dahlia."

He says my name three times before I'm able to take a step back and wipe my face with both hands. His face looks stretched out of shape, viewed through the tears still filling my eyes.

149

"We need to go." He brushes a strand of hair back from my face, where it was plastered to my skin with either tears or snot or both. "And now that you're not crying, we may make it out of the city without being seen."

"How?" Nothing has changed. The city gate will still be locked, and even if it isn't also guarded, neither of us has the clearance to unlock it.

"There's another way out of Lakeview, and as long as they don't know I'm with you they won't know to look for us there. So we have to hurry before they figure that out."

The recall is over. Ford 45 will want to speak to Trigger. About me.

"Wait." Everything is moving too fast. Whatever's wrong with me got my sisters killed, and if I leave Lakeview without that information, I'll never get it. "There's something wrong with me, Trigger. You heard them. I'm an anomaly."

"What I heard is that they haven't found you yet, but now that they've used cadets to double the patrol, they will very, very soon. Come on."

But I pull back on his hand, and he seems even less willing to let go of me than he is to stay in the stairwell.

"I'm different, Trigger." That word has always felt ominous. Different is dangerous. Different is doomed. The recall of my entire genome has more than confirmed that. "No matter how much I look like Poppy and Sorrel and Violet, no matter how much I love them, I never really fit. I've been trying to deny that for a long time. Trying to pretend I don't have thoughts I'm not supposed to have. That I don't want things I'm not supposed to want. But whatever's wrong with me cost my friends their lives, and I have to know what they died for. I have to know how I'm different. I have to know *why* I'm different. I can't strike out into the wild forever without knowing."

My undefined difference would haunt me, along with thousands of ghosts that wear my face.

"Why does it matter?" Trigger asks, and his voice is soft not just in volume but in tone. "You're not different anymore, because there's no one left for you to be different from. Now you are who you are. I *like* who you are. And if we get out of the city, you can be who you are for the rest of your life."

Everything he's saying is true. But . . . "I need to know what's wrong with me and whether this was inevitable," I say. "Were my identicals doomed because of what I am— something beyond my control—or because of what I've done? What *you and I* have done. We're responsible for so much death, Trigger, and I need to know why this is happening. I need to know why I exist in the first place. If I am flawed. I need to know why the geneticist who designed me is on the run just like us." I take a gulp of air. "I need to know how only one out of five thousand identical genomes became flawed, and why he would put that genome into production if he knew."

"Your geneticist is on the run?" Trigger's eyes are wider than I've ever seen them. He's starting to understand.

I nod. "His name is Wexler 42."

"Maybe he didn't know. That's why he's running. He's figured out he made a terrible mistake and that he'll have to pay for that."

A *terrible mistake?* Blood drains from my face, and my cheeks feel cold. Trigger's right. If I wasn't a mistake, none of this would be happening. But the truth still stings.

"No. Wait." He frowns. "That's not what I meant. Wexler 42 made a mistake, obviously, but *you're* not a mistake. In fact, you're kind of a miracle." His gaze intensifies, and I can almost believe him. "The girl who shouldn't exist." His grip tightens around my hand. "You said it yourself; you've always thought differently from the others. If you weren't an anomaly, you probably wouldn't have made it this far."

"If I weren't an anomaly, I wouldn't have needed to. What if I'm sick?"

"What?" His furrowed brow tells me I've finally struck the right chord. "Why would you be sick?"

"Don't they teach history in the Defense Academy? Genetic manipulation began as a way to prevent and eliminate inherited diseases and chromosomal abnormalities. What if whatever's wrong with me is one of those? What if all the other genomes in my union got . . . scrubbed or cleaned or whatever, and they just missed one?"

"I don't think that's how it works, Dahlia. I think they'd have to put a disease into you for it to be there." But he sounds far from sure.

"They're not building genomes from scratch," I explain. "They have to start with base material. There's a vault of genes in the genetics lab. Geneticists start with a sample from the vault and alter it to make sure the people it will produce are healthy, hardy, and well suited to their place. Their union. If the starter genes have flaws, isn't it possible that when they got to me, they just . . . missed something?"

"I don't think so. Wouldn't they scrub the sample, *then* clone it? So that they're all the same? It'd be terribly inefficient to have to scrub each identical's genes individually. . . ."

"But Wexler 42 will know for sure," I insist. "We have to find him. I have to talk to him before we leave."

Trigger exhales slowly. "How long ago did he escape custody?"

There are no clocks in the stairwell, so I can only estimate. "Maybe five minutes before I did. So no more than about three hours ago. Why?"

"I think I know how he'll try to get out of the city," he says, staring at the exterior door as if he can see right through it. Visualizing his plan.

"How?" I wipe my face again, this time with the inside of the jacket I borrowed from Violet. For a second I feel bad about sullying it. Then I remember that she won't need it anymore and I feel even worse. "Another small gate?"

"Not exactly. More like a *special* gate."

"What makes it special?" My toe keeps tapping, and that small sound echoes up through the stairwell. Now that we've decided to go after Wexler, I am full of anxious energy and all out of patience.

"It's only used by certain people, and only at certain times."

What people? What times? How can I know so little about my own city? "How can we get to this special gate without being seen?"

"I have an idea." He opens the exterior door again and peeks through the crack before turning back to me. "Okay. Let's go."

Trigger holds out his hand for me, and I take it as we slip through the doorway. Outside, the sun is finally starting to go down. Shadows are longer now, and I feel a little queasy when I notice that the shade cast by the Specialist Bureau stretches two-thirds of the way to the Defense Bureau. I know that's where we're headed before Trigger even turns in that direction.

I shake my head. "It's too far," I whisper.

"We can make it," he insists just as softly. "Hold your hands behind your back again as if you're still restrained. We're going to march just like we did before, but this time we'll be in the shadow of the building for most of the way."

"What if we're spotted?"

"I don't think we will be. Look." He points between the buildings at some distant point on the grounds, and I follow his finger to see a crowd gathered to watch the tail end of the caravan. "They'll head back inside in a couple of minutes and we'll have lost our shot. Come on."

Before I can argue or even truly think about the risk, he grabs my arm and begins marching with me in tow. I can do nothing without attracting attention except reprise my role from before.

Trigger's form was designed for speed and strength. He moves quickly and I struggle to keep up. But he's right. The rear of the Defense Academy is deserted except for a single black car parked next to the curb on the cruise strip.

"Whose is that?" It looks just like the one that was parked behind the dormitory half an hour ago.

And suddenly I understand. "That's Ford 45's car."

Trigger's jaw is clenched with determination.

"We can't take his car! It won't even start for us." And if anyone other than the owner was to hold a wrist beneath the scanner to try to start it, the car doors would lock and the vehicle would deliver the would-be thief straight to Management headquarters to be arrested.

I remember thinking when I was a child how absurd that standard safety feature was. I couldn't imagine that *anyone* would try to steal a car. That kind of behavior would expose one's genome as being defective.

But that was before I met Trigger 17.

"We're not going to start Ford's car. He is." Trigger heads for the vehicle, and when I don't follow he grabs my hand and pulls me forward again. "We'll just be along for the ride."

"This is . . . *crazy*," I whisper, glancing around as I follow him, certain we're about to be caught. "You want to hitch a ride with the man who organized the slaughter of my entire genome?"

"Yes. He's going to help us escape. I find the irony highly satisfying." His grin swells, and I want to return it, but logic and caution keep getting in the way.

"What if he sees us?" I ask as Trigger pulls open the rear door. Ford 45 has been issued a vehicle that has three rows of seats and will hold eight people. He must be very important indeed.

"He won't even look into the back of the car. Men like Ford 45 rarely take precautions, because they don't have to. Clean clothes show up in his drawer every morning, and there's always food ready to eat at mealtimes. His showers are always hot, and his room is always clean."

"That's true for all of us." Because everyone has a role to fill. We don't see the people who wash our clothes and serve our meals, just like no one sees the hydroponic gardeners who grow our food.

"It's not like that in the wild." Trigger folds the middle row of seats forward and gestures for me to climb over it into the last row. "Or in battle."

Before I can ask whether he's actually been in battle, he climbs in after me. Suddenly we're pressed together on the rear floorboard and all I can think about is how much of his body is touching mine. Dark windows have turned the back of the vehicle into a pool of shadows, and we are suspended in them. Alone together.

Somehow this feels even more intimate and daring than our moments in the equipment shed.

"Are you sure you want to do this?" I am whispering, because the darkness seems to demand it.

"Do what?" Trigger whispers, and I wonder if that's because I whispered first or because the shadows feel delicate to him also. As if too much sound will raise the lights and expose us.

"Run. Escape. You could go back to the dorm right now and tell them you left because you wanted to help with the search. No one will ever know you helped me."

"They'll see you on the security footage eventually," he points out, and I can feel his breath on my cheek with each word. It's a feather of a touch, yet it feels somehow solid. Important. "Besides, we've already been linked through the original arrest record."

"You could tell them you told me to turn myself in. I could hit you on the head so they'd believe I knocked you unconscious."

Trigger chuckles. "They wouldn't believe that even if you were a Special Forces cadet."

"They might," I protest, unable to filter irritation from my voice. "I've become dangerous and unpredictable of late, in case you haven't heard."

His chuckle sounds deeper. More intimate somehow. "I've heard. But if a five-foot-two, one-hundred-ten-pound gardener could knock me unconscious with nothing but her bare fists, I'd deserve to lose my braid."

My eyes widen, but I'm not sure he can see that in the deep shadows. "How do you know my physical dimensions?"

"Special Forces. I'm trained to assess any potential opponent's physical strengths at a glance to better defend myself."

"So? Assess me."

The vehicle rocks slightly as Trigger settles deeper onto

the floorboard, and I hope no one outside has noticed the movement. "Your fingers are nimble and you have excellent fine motor skills. However, your arms are less physically developed than your lower body. That's because you do frequent light lifting and occasional moderate lifting as a part of your primary duty to the city, and you lift with your legs. Your physical recreation consists mostly of team sports concentrating in cardiovascular fitness. A lot of running, like relays and soccer."

"So what am I best suited for?"

"Gardening," Trigger says, and I scowl into the darkness at him.

"I mean, what kind of . . . battle? How much damage could I do in a fight?"

"Against a soldier? Very little. You might get in a lucky kick or two, but your upper body is too weak to pack much of a punch or break someone's hold, and you're too slow to specialize in any of the martial arts that don't require much in the way of size. That can all be fixed, though."

"It can?"

He shrugs. "Somewhat, anyway. You'll never be an extraordinary fighter, because you were designed to grow plants rather than muscles. But your frame is straight and solid, and you could support much more muscle than you currently have. So yeah, you could be taught to defend yourself."

"I—"

Trigger's hand covers my mouth, cutting off my question, and before I can recover from the surprise I hear what he's already heard. Footsteps—boots on concrete. And a voice that is more than familiar after the discussion we overheard on the twelfth floor.

"—want her found within the hour," Ford 45 says. The car rocks around us as he opens the front left door and daylight falls over the interior. We are shielded from the light by the seat backs in front of us, but if either Ford or the soldier he's talking to looks through the rear window, he will see us. "Ping me immediately when you have her. You have my direct contact?"

Through the tinted glass, I see the other man nod. The name on his uniform is Calibre 32.

Ford closes the door and I peek between the seats to see him holding his wrist beneath the sensor built into the dashboard. The engine hums to life and the car vibrates around us. Ford leans his seat back and pulls a small tablet from his inner suit pocket. "The Administrator's mansion," he says as he begins tapping and swiping his way through a series of messages I can't read.

The car rolls forward smoothly, following the cruise strip painted onto the road, and I rock with the motion, surprised when my stomach seems to lag behind the rest of my body for a second. I've never been in a vehicle before. In fact, I rarely even see cars, because the training ward is populated mostly by children and adolescents, who lack the authority to start a CityCar.

Not that we'd have anywhere to go if we could start one.

The screen built into the dashboard shows the default

route as a highlighted line through a two-dimensional map of the city. I stare at it for as long as I dare, fascinated, but Ford doesn't even glance at it. He's already lost in his leadership duties.

As the private vehicle rounds the dormitory and rolls onto the main road, daylight falls on Trigger's face and I realize that he isn't terrified by Ford's destination as I am. Instead he looks relieved. He *wants* to go to the Administrator's mansion.

And somehow he knew that's exactly where Ford 45 would take us.

FOURTEEN

I stare out the window over Trigger's head as familiar buildings steadily march past at an unfamiliar angle. I've never seen them like this. So tall and . . . fleeting.

A chime rings through the vehicle and I flinch, startled by the sudden sound. The dashboard screen flashes, and the map of our route disappears to reveal a message reading *Incoming communication request.*

"Accept," Ford 45 says.

The screen flashes again and I catch a glimpse of a lightly lined female face and graying hair pulled back into a Management-style bun as I duck back behind the seat, my heart pounding in fear.

Trigger's eyes are wide. *Were you seen?* his expression seems to demand.

I shake my head. And hope I'm right.

"Administrator," Ford 45 says. "I'm on my way—"

"Where is she?" the Administrator demands.

My throat feels tight. They're talking about me.

"I believe we're closing in on her—"

"You *believe*? I want to hear what you know. Do you *know* where she is?"

"No, ma'am. I'm on my way to the mansion, then I'm headed back to the Defense Academy to question the cadet. I—"

"Ford 45, that girl represents the greatest security threat Lakeview has ever seen." The Administrator's declaration sends chills across my skin.

"But she's just a gardener," Ford says, echoing my own thoughts. "What's so dangerous about a defective gard—"

"She *cannot* escape the city. What about the geneticist?"

"Wexler 42. He's still missing. His lab is studying the genome, trying to figure out what happened with Dahlia 16, but the whole thing is very strange, ma'am. They can't find any of the DNA assembly records and work logs for the genome in question."

During the Administrator's brief silence, I can hear my own heartbeat.

"You think Wexler 42 deleted them?" she asks at last.

"Defense has its best digital forensics team on it, and so far they haven't found any sign that the records were deleted." Ford 45's seat creaks as he shifts uncomfortably. "They can't find any sign that the records ever existed in the first place."

"That's not possible. Protocol demands a record of every gene in the sequence."

"Yes, ma'am. The digital team couldn't find the city's original commission for the year-sixteen trade labor class. I'm headed to the mansion to search for it in backup storage. Then I'll—"

"You better be here in five minutes. And, Ford 45?"

"Yes, Administrator?"

"If you don't find both the geneticist and the anomaly *today*, I will promote someone else to Bureau Chief and have *you* recalled." Another chime signals the end of the communication.

Stunned, I can only stare at Trigger, trying to decide based on his equally shocked expression whether he understood more of that than I did.

Ford groans. Then I hear a loud crack and a gasp of pain. I peek between the seats to see that the screen has been shattered and the knuckles of Ford 45's right hand are dripping blood.

Obviously he doesn't want to be recalled either.

Seconds later the car rolls to a smooth stop. I frown and twist quietly to look through the window over my head. We only left the training ward a few minutes ago. How can we already have arrived at the Administrator's mansion? Is the city so small that I could have walked across it if I'd had permission?

Between the seats, I see Ford slide his tablet back into his suit jacket pocket with his clean left hand. He opens the door and steps out of the car, holding his bleeding right hand close to his chest.

Through the window over my head, I watch him walk away from the vehicle without even a glance back, but I can't see where he's going without revealing myself.

Trigger is right. Ford's carelessness comes from a kind of arrogance I've never even considered. He assumes that everyone else lacks the intelligence or the audacity to breach his personal space and property, because he's in a position of authority and no longer spends his time surrounded by his few identicals. And for the most part he's right. It would never have occurred to me to hitch a ride in the rear of his personal vehicle. To make my escape by sticking close to the very man trying to catch me.

Trigger puts one hand on my arm and I turn to see him making a shushing gesture with one finger over his lips. I nod and he sits taller, slowly, until he can peer through the glass over my head to make sure no one's around to see us get out of the car. He's counting on the tinted windows—and a little bit of luck—to shield him from sight, and I'm happy to let him take that risk for both of us, even though if he's seen, we're both caught.

"There are two men waiting by the door," he whispers. "They can't see into the car, if you want to look."

I don't want to look, but if I'm going to make it out of the city—if I'm going to survive in the wild—I have to start taking more risks. So I turn in the narrow space until I can rise on my knees and look through the window.

We're behind a building I've never seen before. It isn't a tower like the Workforce Academy or the dormitory. It isn't a squat building like the Defense Academy or a shiny building like Management headquarters. This building is short—only three stories high—with quaint windows and great peaks of roof covered in vintage tar shingles.

It's the roof that clues me in. This isn't a public building. It's a private residence. A swollen version of the individual homes we learned about during our history unit, from back when people were born rather than grown and lived in family units consisting of genetic siblings and the parents who conceived them.

"This is a *house*," I whisper, and the words sound as confused as I feel.

"The only one in the city," Trigger confirms. "It's the Administrator's mansion."

"Why does the Administrator need a giant house?" I share—*shared*—a room and clothing with three other people. A classroom and supplies with more than a dozen. A cafeteria with hundreds. A face with thousands.

"It's not just a house. She works out of the mansion, running the city, meeting with the bureau chiefs and with representatives of other cities and doing whatever else an Administrator does."

"How many rooms does she need for that?" My gaze tracks up the rear of the mansion, over brick and stone and what appear to be painted slats of wood. There are three chimneys and one large open area where three black private vehicles are parked. "Why does one woman need three cars?"

"I think most of that is less a need than a privilege." But I can tell from the distracted quality of Trigger's voice that he's no longer interested in the Administrator's mansion. "They're going in."

I follow his gaze to see Ford 45 enter the house through a rear door. A man in black pants and a black shirt steps in after him, while another dressed just like the first holds the door open, then lets it close as he follows them inside.

"Who are those men?" I whisper as Trigger rises onto his knees to look more boldly through all the car windows.

"Private security. They were recruited from Special Forces to protect high-ranking officials like the bureau chiefs and the Administrator."

"Protect them from what?"

Trigger blinks. His brow furrows, as if that question has never occurred to him before. "I don't know. Threats from outside the city, I guess."

"What kind of threats?"

Trigger settles into the seat and frowns down at me. "For a girl who never asked a question in her life before a couple of months ago, you sure do have a lot of them now." He crawls between the two middle seats in front of us and reaches for the door. "We need to go while no one's watching."

I crawl after him and stare at the windows sparsely distributed across the back of the Administrator's mansion. "If anyone looks out, we're caught."

"Yes. So move fast." Trigger brushes past me and steps out of the car. I follow him out onto a slab of concrete into which

166

intricate, whirling designs have been pressed. He closes the car door softly, then reaches for my hand again, and suddenly we are running.

His boots make no sound on the concrete, but my athletic shoes are not as quiet, and I'm so busy trying to imitate his silence that at first I don't realize we're running toward the mansion rather than away from it.

"Wait!" I pull him to a stop halfway across the Administrator's back patio. This is incredibly dangerous. We could be seen at any second. But going into the mansion seems so crazy that for a second I wonder if his real goal is—"Trigger?" Something in my voice makes him turn, and he seems to understand my fear with one glance at my face.

"I'm not turning you in, Dahlia. If that was what I wanted, I would have just let the Commander catch you in the dorm."

"Why are you helping me?" In that moment, despite the danger of being caught, I have to know.

Trigger presses a quick kiss against my lips. "Because I like you. I don't want to lose you." His small smile makes my insides feel warm. "And because I want to see just how deep your wild roots will grow. So *come on*," he whispers, tugging me into motion again.

Against my better judgment, we cross the rest of the patio toward the room full of cars. Distant memory of past history lessons labels it a "garage," but I still can't fathom one woman's need for so many different vehicles.

I follow Trigger into the garage, where I see that there isn't a speck of dust on any of the cars; then he takes a sharp left and pulls open another door. Behind it a flight of stairs leads down into the dark. He motions for me to proceed, then closes the door at his back and we are alone in the dark. Again.

"Where are we?"

"Shh." He brushes past me and his touch trails down my arm until he finds my hand, which he places firmly on the rail attached to the wall, obscured by the darkness. "We can't risk turning on a light until we're farther from the house. The stairs are steep. Be careful." His footsteps echo as they descend, headed away from me.

I feel my way slowly, and when his steps end I realize he's stopped at the bottom of the flight to wait for me. His hand finds mine again when my shoes hit concrete.

"There's a light up here a few feet, if I'm remembering this correctly." He tugs me forward, and I hear the brush of his hand against the wall to our right. Something clicks, then soft light from about twenty feet ahead illuminates the concrete tunnel around us.

"Where are we?" I ask as I follow him through the tunnel.

"The Administrator's emergency exit."

"But we're already out of her house." My sneakers shuffle against the dusty concrete as I try to keep up with Trigger.

"It's so she can exit the city, not the house."

"Why does the Administrator need an emergency exit? What kind of emergency?"

"Any kind, I guess."

We pass beneath the first bulb, and when Trigger flips the

next switch, the bulb we've passed is extinguished as the one ahead lights up.

"So this tunnel leads to the city gate?"

"One of them." His voice seems to bounce back at us from every surface of the narrow tunnel. "It's the VIP gate. For very important people. There aren't many of those, so the gate isn't used much."

"And you think that's where we'll find Wexler?" Or is this his way of bypassing my request altogether? *Oh, well, your geneticist isn't here, but since we are, we might as well strike off into the wild. . . .*

"That's my best guess, if he's still in the city."

"How would he even know about this gate? Are geneticists that important?" Yet I know the answer before I've even finished asking. Without geneticists, humanity would have to go back to the old, messy, inefficient way of producing children who might die of inherited diseases and would certainly never live up to their potential, being made of random strands of DNA rather than handpicked genes ideally suited for a specific purpose.

The world as we know it would collapse without geneticists.

"Yes," Trigger says, confirming my thoughts. "Every year the Administrator sends a delegate of Management leaders and geneticists out of Lakeview to meet with representatives from several other cities. They call it a summit. At his age, Wexler 42 has probably attended several times, and he would have left the city through the gate we're headed for, which also happens to be the Administrator's personal emergency exit. Since it's only occasionally used, it's not regularly guarded, so it's Wexler's best chance of getting out. Not coincidentally it now represents our best chance as well."

"Is this the way you were going to take me before I told you about Wexler?"

"No. I was going to introduce you to the wonderland that is the Lakeview city sewer system. But since we're headed for the VIP gate, we'll give that a shot first."

"How do you know all this, Trigger?" And how much more is there that I *don't* know?

"We don't all spend every day in a plant lab surrounded by tubers. The last two years of a cadet's training is fifty percent 'in the field.' We participate in drills aimed to prepare us for every possible kind of emergency as well as to determine what positions we'll be most useful in after graduation."

"It's much the same for gardeners," I tell him as I flip a switch to turn on a light up ahead. "Those best at apples and pears will grow fruit trees. Those best at yams and potatoes will grow tubers. But we have to try everything to know what we're best at."

"Exactly. A couple of months ago, my squad trained for VIP guard duty. If we're permanently assigned to that field, there'll be much more training in my future."

He's speaking in the future tense, as if he's forgotten that where we are and what we're doing will forever alter the trajectory of our lives. Assuming we live.

I decide not to point that out.

"But as a year-seventeen Special Forces cadet, I've had a little bit of training in a lot of highly sensitive areas."

"This is why they don't want commingling between different bureaus," I whisper as we near the edge of the current circle of light.

Trigger stops long enough to grin at me, his gaze caught on mine, and heat pools low in my stomach. "That's only *one* of the reasons they don't want girls like you mingling with guys like me."

I don't know what to say to that. This feeling I have for him—this attraction—is still so new I don't know if it can be trusted. It's so unexpectedly physical, and somehow similar to both winning an exhilarating relay *and* catching a stomach bug. The way he looks at me sends pleasant chills down my spine, yet my palms are slick with sweat. I want it to stop so I can think straight, yet I never want it to end.

Were girls in the archaic time of bodily fluids and congenital disease so mixed up and confused?

I think about that while we walk, flipping switches as we go, so that only one portion of the concrete tunnel is lit at any given time. I have no way to judge the distance, but my best guess is that we've been walking for half an hour when we see another set of stairs, this one leading aboveground.

"There shouldn't be anyone here," Trigger 17 says as we ascend. "But be quiet just in case."

I follow him out of the tunnel and into a long, tall stone passageway, which curves gradually in each direction. "Where are we?" I whisper as my gaze roams over the dusty passage, so different from the stark, polished surfaces and clean lines of my academy and dormitory.

"Inside the city wall," he whispers in return.

"Why is it hollow?"

"Because a city wall isn't as simple as the wall of a building. It has to be thicker. Stronger. It doesn't just define the edge of Lakeview; it defends the city from anything on the other side."

Yet in my lifetime, Lakeview has not been in need of defense, that I know of. Was that different in the past? Did we have enemies determined to breach such a barrier?

"This wall is twelve feet thick and twenty feet tall, and it's hollow on the inside to allow for the movement of troops and supplies regardless of the conditions outside. We've come up in the middle, so we've bypassed the locked gate that lets people inside the wall. But there's another up ahead. That one actually leads out of the city."

"Can you open it?" I ask.

"We're about to find out."

"What does that mean?"

"That means that a camera feed is one thing, but I doubt my basic electronic systems unit gave me sufficient skills to hack the VIP gate. But I'm going to give it a shot."

Yet after several minutes and a series of dimly lit wall sconces, no gate appears. Finally Trigger stops walking.

"What's wrong?" I glance back the way we came. "Are we going the wrong way?"

He shakes his head. "We can't be." But he turns to follow my gaze anyway. "I could have *sworn* the gate was to the left. We should have found it by now."

"Well, unless they've moved it, I think we went the wrong way."

"But we didn't," he insists. "I patrolled this section of the wall for an entire week. Let's just round that curve, and if the gate isn't there we'll go back."

Yet before we even get to the curve, laughter echoes toward us from some point beyond it.

Trigger freezes. His eyes close. "That's the patrol break room," he whispers. "The *break room* was left. The gate was right."

"We all make mistakes." *Evidently.* I take his hand and try to pull him back the way we came, but he stands his ground, staring in the direction of the laughter.

"I didn't think there'd be anyone patrolling right now. We're a month away from the summit."

"You can't know everything that happens in Lakeview, Trigger."

"Yes, but I checked the security status using my instructor's clearance and there was nothing listed. Whatever's going on here, Defense officially knows nothing about it."

"Even more reason we should get moving. Come on," I whisper fiercely, tugging on his hand now.

He takes one step backward. Then we both go still as footsteps echo toward us from around the curve.

"Too late," Trigger mumbles. "Stay put."

"Why?" I ask as he retreats into shadow, where the light from one sconce doesn't quite meet the light from the next. A second later a soldier rounds the curve. Only he isn't a typical patrol soldier. He's wearing all black—like the Administrator's private security.

The soldier stops when he sees me, and his hand hovers over the gun strapped to the belt at his waist. "Who are . . . ?" He steps closer, and his gaze focuses on my face. "Oh." His hand falls away from his gun. "What are you . . . ?"

Trigger appears silently in the shadows behind him, a silhouette against what little light falls on the passage inside the city's wall. Before the soldier can turn, Trigger wraps one arm around his neck and squeezes, applying extra pressure by gripping his own wrist with his free hand.

The soldier claws at Trigger's arm, but within seconds his face turns an alarming shade of red. His eyes roll into his head and his arms go slack. When his legs fold beneath him, Trigger drags the poor man into the deepest shadows against the wall.

"I don't think he was going to shoot me," I whisper as Trigger ushers me back the way we came.

"Of course not." We pass through the light from one fixture into the light of the next, our footsteps nearly silent on the stone floor. "The Administrator wants you alive."

"No, I mean he didn't seem like a threat."

"You're wrong about that. Only the deadliest Special

Forces soldiers are recruited for private security." His pause feels strangely heavy. "That was my ambition."

"I'm sorry." I've pulled him from the life of honor and distinction he was supposed to have.

"Don't be. There's something exciting about not knowing what's next. Don't you think? Something exhilarating."

I'm not sure I *do* think that. As much as I like the idea of picking wild vegetables, I also liked knowing when and where I would get my next meal. I liked sitting with Poppy in the cafeteria, trading my corn for her tomatoes.

It's dinnertime, and I don't know how to find food now that I'm not supposed to exist, either in Lakeview or in the wild. And I don't have Poppy.

"I wonder what's going on?" Trigger mumbles as we walk, and I realize he's lost in thoughts of his own. "That private soldier—I recognized his genome. He graduated when I was a year fourteen. If all the soldiers in the break room were private security, something big must be going on. . . ."

We slow down after we pass the Administrator's secret tunnel, and Trigger starts to look more confident. "Yes. This is the way. Sorry for the detour."

I can't resist a small smile. "It's good to know you're not right *all* the time."

"Why would that be good to—"

A soft scraping noise draws us both to a startled stop. He raises one finger to his lips, but I'm already too scared to make a sound, other than the thunder of my heartbeat in my ears.

Trigger holds one palm out in a "wait here" gesture, but my feet don't want to listen. I don't even realize I'm still following him—*finally* I've mastered silent steps—until over his shoulder I see a man wearing a long white lab coat. He's hunched over a scanner built into the stone wall next to a massive, reinforced metal door. The man turns, and I recognize him.

We've found both the runaway geneticist *and* the city gate.

FIFTEEN

"Wexler 42!" His name explodes from my mouth before I even feel it on my tongue, and when Trigger flinches I realize I've shouted. The geneticist looks up as his name bounces back at me from every surface of the stone tunnel. Our gazes meet. His expression shuffles through surprise, then relief. He's not happy to see me, but he's not frightened by my presence either.

Trigger, however . . .

"Who's your friend?" Wexler demands as his gaze rakes over the cadet, apparently searching for weapons.

Friend. My eyes close and Poppy's smile flashes across my memory. I've never used the term *friend* to refer to anyone who doesn't look just like me, but this new use of the word feels less strange than it might have before Trigger's non-traditional use of words like *beautiful* and *kiss.*

"This is Trigger 17." There's no reason to withhold that information, because his felonious aiding and abetting has probably already been discovered by Management. He's probably as wanted as I am.

That, and if we come a few feet closer he'll be able to read Trigger's name on his uniform.

"Trigger." Wexler seems to be tasting the name. Trying it out. "The toy soldier who woke up Sleeping Beauty. Too bad the world will never hear that story."

My brow furrows. I don't understand.

Wexler laughs, and his gaze has caught on me now. "He's the boy from the shed, right?"

Of course he knows about the shed. They would have told him what I'd done when they asked him what was wrong with my genome.

"But that wasn't the first time, was it? Before the equipment shed, he was the boy from the elevator, right?" My surprise must be obvious, because he chuckles again. "It's in your files. An alert went out for Trigger 17 twenty minutes ago, so I cross-checked his name with yours." Wexler holds up his tablet.

Why would he ask me Trigger's name if he already knew it? Did he think I would lie?

"Why aren't they tracking you through that?" Trigger's gaze is focused on the tablet. When Wexler doesn't answer, Trigger frowns. "They should have been all over you the minute you logged in to the system. Did you disable the locator?"

I have no idea what he's talking about, but the geneticist doesn't look confused.

"He hacked his tablet." Trigger turns back to Wexler before I can figure out which question to ask first. "Can you hack the door lock?" He sounds excited now, as if escape is suddenly a real possibility.

"I'm trying." Wexler turns back to the wrist scanner, which is mounted to the wall at an odd angle. "But it seems to be less an issue of hacking than . . . snipping." He pulls a small folding knife from his pocket with his spare hand.

No, it's not mounted. The scanner is now *hanging* from the wall, shining its red laser beam at the floor near our feet. Wexler has pulled it away from its base panel to expose a smaller panel connecting several colored wires to several other wires.

"No!" Trigger pushes him out of the way. "Cutting any of the wires will trigger an alarm. You have to access it through the system. Give me that." He snatches Wexler's tablet and begins scrolling and tapping his way through options so fast I don't have a chance to read them.

Gardeners have access to a class set of tablets for schoolwork, yet I don't recognize anything I'm seeing on Wexler's. I don't know what system they're talking about.

While Trigger works on hacking, I grab the geneticist's arm, and with it his attention. Wexler returns my gaze not as if he wants to look at me, but as if he *has* to. As if he can't help it. "What's wrong with me?" I demand before I can lose my nerve. "With my genome?"

"You are an anomaly."

"I know that!" My hand clenches around his elbow. "But what does it mean?"

"There's nothing wrong with you." Wexler pulls his arm from my grip and takes a step back. "You're just . . . different."

Panic burns its way up my throat. "I can't be different. *No one's* different." Different means inefficient and conspicuous. Different is a death sentence. "Ford 45 said—"

"You spoke to Ford?" Wexler's brown eyes widen as Trigger grumbles softly at the tablet, and even in the dim light from a bulb ten feet above us I can see the tension in every line of his aging face.

"No. We overheard him talking to one of the Defense commanders. He said I have two defects. What are they? Why can't I see them?"

"First of all, they're not defects. They're anomalies," Wexler insists. I open my mouth to argue, but he speaks over me. "And second, you can't see them because they're on a genetic level. They're only visible with a very powerful microscope, and even then they're only obvious with twenty-five years of genetics training. Physically you are virtually identical to all the other girls in your division."

"Virtually? Not exactly? Did you put flaws into my genome on purpose? Or did you just forget to fix mine before I was put into production?"

But he's already talking again, following his own thoughts rather than mine. "They're not flaws, Dahlia. You have no flaws. You are *perfect.* I made sure of that."

Pride echoes as clearly in his voice as indignation shines in his eyes. He's insulted by the description of something he created as "flawed." Yet how can any difference not be a defect?

"You don't understand." His gaze searches mine. "But that's not because you *can't* understand. It's because they've taught that possibility right out of you. It's a shortcoming of nurture, not nature." His focus strays from my eyes until he's watching all of me. Studying me. The attention feels invasive yet not personal. He's looking at me like I look at my best tomato plants, as if he's pleased with the work he's done. "You are unique, Dahlia."

Trigger glances up from the tablet in surprise, and I realize he's been listening even as he taps and swipes his way toward freedom.

Unique. That word burns into me like the heat in the center of a chunk of coal. I feel like I will crack into fiery bits at any moment.

Unique comes from the root of the word *one*. It means individual. Distinctive. Singular. One of a kind. The *only* of its kind. I know the definition, yet the concept feels obscure and out of focus. Not relevant to me or to anything I've ever known.

No one is unique. Geneticists are few, but they are not unique. Trigger is scarred, but beneath the marks training has given him, he is the same as all his identicals, down to the basic building blocks of life.

Even the Administrator . . .

Well, the Administrator *is* unique, but only because the

rest of her genome was "retired." Because Lakeview only needs one Administrator. But even she didn't start off as an individual. To make her unique, they had to euthanize everyone else created from her genome.

Because I'm unique, they euthanized everyone else created from my genome.

For the Administrator, being unique is an honor she's earned. But for me it is a disaster. A death sentence. Why would a sixteen-year-old hydroponic gardener—one of thousands of laborers—be different from the rest? How did it happen?

"You knew." I can hear the accusation in my voice, and Wexler doesn't deny the charge. "You knew I was flawed, but you put me into production anyway. Why?"

"It's not that simple. You're not a clone, Dahlia."

"*What?*" Trigger looks up from the tablet. His brow is furrowed. "Everyone's a clone."

"Not Dahlia. She's a prototype. The mold from which the others were all formed. But she wasn't supposed to be."

"I don't understand what that means." In fact, I don't understand anything anymore. How can anyone be unique? And . . . "If I'm a prototype, shouldn't I be like all the others? Or rather, shouldn't they all be like me?"

"Usually, yes." Wexler runs one hand through his short hair, then exhales heavily. "They'll kill us all if they catch us, so you may as well know the truth. Dahlia, your genome was never meant to be cloned."

"That makes no sense," Trigger says, just as I say, "What *was* it meant for?"

"You were a special order for a private client from another city. An under-the-table order, because we're not allowed to work for anything other than the glory of Lakeview. As you well know."

"Client?" I don't know that word. "Under the table?" It's like he's speaking another language.

"Years ago, I did a favor for a friend from another city. But I had to do the work in secret."

"I was that work?"

"Yes. And I was *very* proud of the work I did on you." Wexler is watching me like a tomato again, eyeing my every feature. Studying my every gesture. "But engineering you took so long I no longer had time to do my actual job. I had no choice but to alter your genome slightly to fit Lakeview's needs, then use that tweaked version to fulfill Management's order for five thousand female trade laborers."

For one long moment, his words tumble around in my head, refusing to line up in any order that makes sense. Until finally one fact emerges from the chaos. "You designed me for another city?"

"That's *treason*," Trigger snaps with more anger than seems fitting for a boy currently trying to disable the lock on one of the city gates.

Wexler ignores him. "Not for a city. For a person."

"Who?" Why would anyone need a genome?

183

"That doesn't matter, and you wouldn't understand the answer," Wexler insists.

My cheeks burn with anger, but I move on because I am suddenly very aware of how long we've been here and how close Management might be to finding us. "You designed me for a *person*, then you tweaked my genome and used it to produce an entire class of trade laborers for the city of Lakeview?"

Wexler nods.

"And those tweaks are the differences between my genome and all the others?"

"Yes!" He's clearly excited that I am catching on. He looks . . . proud. "And you are everything you were supposed to be. If anyone is 'flawed,' it's the others. Your 'identicals.'"

But that makes no sense. None of the others were caught kissing a boy they had no business even speaking to. None of the others are running for their lives. None of the others have condemned thousands of their sisters to a hopefully peaceful but very permanent death.

"Why am I here if you designed me for a person in another city? Why didn't you fulfill the order?"

"I did fulfill it!" But Wexler's gaze drops to the ground. "At least, I thought I did." He fiddles with the edge of his lab coat, and I wonder why he's still wearing such a distinctive garment while he's on the run. "But when they showed me the result of your blood test, I recognized my own work immediately. It seems that I accidentally sent one of the genetically altered embryos—one of your clones—to fulfill the private order."

"And I—the prototype—wound up as one of five thousand trade laborers who are only identical to me on the outside."

"Yes." Wexler nods absently, as if he's lost in his own thoughts. "That's the only explanation that makes sense."

Yet somehow *none* of this makes sense. Talk of unique individuals and private orders means little to me other than a vague, uneasy awareness of how very wrong the whole thing feels. How very strange and illogical and incredibly inefficient.

Why design only one of anything?

What use would anyone have for one child? A child who is *unique*, as far as Wexler's friend from another city knows. What happened to that girl I was supposed to be? Why would she be raised alone? Is she being trained to be something special? Like . . . an Administrator?

"What are these tweaks?" I ask as Trigger types something into a form on Wexler's tablet. "What makes me different from all the others?"

"It's nothing you will ever need to worry about. You have my word."

"I'm not . . . sick?"

The geneticist looks appalled. "No. You are perfect." He glances at his tablet and his eyes narrow when he sees what's on the screen. Whatever hacking Trigger has managed to do. "Here." He snatches the tablet over the cadet's protests and

185

opens a new screen. His fingers move so fast I can barely follow the motions, and a couple of seconds later he pulls a familiar penlike device from one of the pockets of his lab coat. "Give me your finger. I'll show you the differences."

I hold out my hand, and Wexler's pen bites into the fleshy part of my middle finger and takes its sample. A red bubble wells up on my finger and I stare at it, fascinated that something as small as a single drop—not to mention a chain of DNA—can tell the world so much about a person.

Wexler pulls the cap off the opposite end of his pen to reveal a small bit of metal. He plugs the pen into his tablet and a fresh screen opens. Seconds and a few taps later, Wexler holds the tablet out so I can see it. He taps and scrolls his way through charts and images—chromosomes, a DNA helix, and several things I can't even identify—so quickly that I can hardly focus on the first before it's gone. He speaks as quickly as he swipes, and I recognize even fewer of the genetics terms than I do the images; I'm relieved to see that Trigger looks as mystified as I feel.

"But what does all that *mean?*" the cadet demands when Wexler scrolls into the dozenth image in just a few minutes.

The geneticist launches into a brand-new "simplified" version of his explanation, and Trigger and I focus so much of our attention on the images and words that we don't notice the approaching noise until it's nearly upon us.

Trigger hears it first, and when he looks up from the tablet, his narrow-eyed gaze focused in the direction of the Administrator's secret escape passage, adrenaline fires through my veins. The sound is just a scrape against concrete, but I recognize it as footsteps. Several sets.

"What did you *do?*" Trigger demands, and I turn to see that he has Wexler by the throat. The tablet no longer shows confusing charts and illustrations. Instead Wexler has re-opened the screen Trigger was last on and has entered several characters into a form that has replaced them with asterisks to hide the password from us.

"How *could* you?" I whisper as the truth hits me. I should have realized he didn't need a new sample, since there was already one on file. "Trigger, he took my blood because he knew that would sound an alert."

Wexler gurgles something inarticulate that seems to support my guess.

"It's only been minutes," Trigger whispers. "Not enough time to move troops in bulk. These must have come straight from the Administrator's mansion."

"In bulk?" I feel like I'm going to be sick. "How many will they send?"

"If they know I'm with you? Plenty. But I only hear three sets so far." He lets go of Wexler's throat. "Open the door. Now."

Wexler inhales in great gulps, hunched over his tablet as he struggles to catch his breath. "Trigger is their worst night-mare," he gasps. "They've taught him enough to make him truly dangerous."

The same seems to be true of the geneticist, but in a completely different way.

"Open it," Trigger growls. "Now." Then he takes off in the direction of the approaching footsteps just as three uniformed soldiers round the curve.

Wexler raises his tablet and types frantically with one hand. Trigger throws his foot in a wide arching kick, knocking guns away from two of the three soldiers at once. And I can only watch, fascinated, while each of them fights for our freedom in his own way, hoping that my skills will prove more useful in the wild.

Trigger drops to the ground and sweeps one soldier's feet from beneath him while he grasps for one of the dropped guns. He stands, weapon in hand, and bashes the fallen soldier in the head with the grip of the weapon. The soldier collapses in a heap at his identicals' feet.

On my right, Wexler makes a gleeful sound, and I turn to see that his password has been accepted and he's being asked to confirm some command.

Trigger grunts again, and I spin just as one of the disarmed soldiers punches him in the jaw. His head snaps back and he stumbles into the wall behind him. Trigger bounces back to jab the soldier in the gut, then grabs the man's head and rams it into the stone wall once, twice, three times. The soldier falls and Trigger stands up straight to face his only remaining foe.

Red light flashes in my eyes and a high-pitched electronic wailing scrapes the inside of my skull raw. But beneath that is a low grinding sound. I turn back to Wexler and find the huge metal door slowly rolling open. My heart leaps into my throat. Whatever password he's stolen has unlocked the gate but set off an alarm.

"Stop him!" Trigger yells as the geneticist tries to squeeze through the slowly widening crack between the door and the wall. The warning costs him another punch to the face, but then he's up and jabbing again, balancing nimbly on the balls of his feet, as if this is a dance rather than a fight for our lives. "We need him to close the door again or they'll follow us!"

I spin again and pull Wexler back from the opening, glad he's too wide to fit through yet. In his eyes I find fear and unapologetic triumph, but no guilt. He knew opening the door would set off an alarm and draw soldiers down from the top of the wall. He also knew that fighting Trigger would keep the soldiers occupied long enough for him to escape.

He's sacrificed us for his own freedom.

Well, he tried to, anyway.

"You can't leave us!" I shout, pulling him farther from the door. "This is your fault!" He's bigger than I am, but I am determined. I need him for more than just closing the door once we've escaped. I still have questions only he can answer.

"Dahlia, your fate was sealed before you were ever born. I am sorry about the mix-up, though. Sad to think what might have been."

I clutch his arm in both of mine and pull him farther from the door. But then I feel the fabric slip. He's already shrugged out of the first sleeve of his lab coat and is pulling free from the other one, even as I cling to it.

"No!" I shout as I lose my grasp on his arm. He bolts for

the opening and I scramble for a new grip. My nails gouge into his wrist. Blood wells from the scratches and drips onto the floor. Then Wexler is gone.

I turn to yell for Trigger, but he's already running toward me. All three of the soldiers lie on the floor unconscious. "Let's go!" he shouts.

But the thunder of footsteps nearly drowns out his words. The fading daylight falling through the open door is suddenly obscured, and I turn to see five more soldiers blocking the gate. Behind them, coming from the direction of the Administrator's private tunnel, are three more.

We are outnumbered. We are outgunned. Trigger's hands are in the air.

I can see the wild over the soldiers' shoulders. Tall trees crowned in brightly colored fall leaves, growing right out of the dirt. Grass and weeds and flowers sprouting from the earth itself with no defined borders or geometric patterns. Wind blows, and the leaves brush together with a full-bodied whispering sound; I want nothing more than to climb into the branches and sing with the bright foliage.

Someone grabs my hands and binds them at my back. Tears fill my eyes. Trigger is unconscious, a lump already growing on the side of his head while two soldiers haul him away, each holding one of his arms.

As they drag me toward examination and certain death, my gaze returns to the trees, the flowers, and the weeds.

The wild is so close. Yet I've never felt farther from it in my life.

SIXTEEN

The soldiers put us in the back of a patrol car. Trigger is still unconscious, and a line of blood has dripped down from his temple over his ear. I wonder if he will have a new scar.

I wonder if he will live long enough for it to remind him of me.

A click echoes in my head as the rear doors of the car are locked. There's no handle on the inside. I couldn't get out even if I had the use of my hands.

"Trigger," I whisper as two of the soldiers get into the front of the car. "Trigger. Wake up. Please."

"He can't help you anymore," Gladius 27, one of the soldiers, says from the front right seat. "He can't even help himself."

"Administrator's mansion," the other soldier says, holding his wrist beneath the sensor built into the dashboard. "Rear entrance."

"The mansion?" Gladius asks as Trigger's eyelids begin to flutter.

"Ford 45 said no one can see her. The rest of her division has already been recalled, and if people find out she escaped, Management's effectiveness will come into question—which would undermine the Administrator's ability to lead."

My chest feels too tight. I can't draw a breath. Poppy and the others are gone, but hearing about it reopens a wound that hasn't even started to heal.

"This capture will best serve the city in secrecy," the other soldier continues.

"Strategic omission," I murmur, thinking back to one of my first conversations with Trigger. "Anything necessary to protect the city is permissible."

Both soldiers twist in their seats to look at me as the car follows the road toward the Administrator's mansion. Gladius's partner is named Pike 27. They are from the same division. Maybe from the same unit. "What else has he told you?" Pike asks with a glance at Trigger, whose head has fallen forward.

"Does it matter? They'll kill me before I have a chance to tell anyone."

I don't recognize the bitter truth in my statement until I hear it come from my mouth. If I wasn't going to die, *would* I tell someone what I know about the Defense Bureau? Who would I tell?

Poppy is gone. Even if she wasn't, knowing what I know would put her in danger.

The irony of that thought bruises me all the way into my soul.

The soldiers shrug at each other, then turn to face forward again, effectively dismissing me.

I hardly notice the unfamiliar buildings on either side of the road, because Trigger's eyes are still moving behind his closed lids. He could wake up any second, and that second cannot come soon enough.

"Trigger!" I whisper again, and finally his eyelids stay up. His eyes focus on me, then they widen. I can practically see the past half hour coming back to him as memories sift into place.

"I'm so sorry, Dahlia." His speech is slurred. That happened to Violet once, when her head got between a soccer ball and the goal. She was fine within the hour.

I'm not sure Trigger and I can afford that hour.

"Where are we going?" he asks.

I nod at the building approaching through the windshield. "Back to the mansion."

"*Back* to the mansion?" Gladius 27 twists in his seat to look at us.

Trigger chuckles, and I think that means he's feeling better. "We caught a ride with Ford 45 from the Defense Academy."

Both soldiers mumble harsh syllables I don't recognize, and I realize that neither wants to be the bearer of that bit of intelligence.

Following the cruise strip, the car turns before we reach the front of the mansion and circles the building to the very lot where we snuck out of Ford's car less than an hour ago. Everything looks a little different now that the sun is going down. The shadows are deeper and darker. The light is redder.

I wonder how much easier it would be to sneak around the city in the dark. I'm pretty sure I won't get the chance to find out.

The car slows to a stop, and Trigger lets Gladius 27 pull him from the vehicle. I step out on my own before Pike can haul me out, but he grabs my arm the moment I'm on my feet.

The soldiers lead us through the rear entrance of the mansion, then down a narrow back hallway into a large cell containing nothing except a concrete bench built into the wall. Both soldiers station themselves outside the open door, effectively blocking our escape, and warn us that they were told to bring us in alive but not necessarily conscious.

The threat is clear.

Trigger studies the room in narrow-eyed concentration. If he's been taught to assess his opponents at a glance, I'm pretty sure he's also been taught to assess his surroundings, and I'm hopeful that he sees some point of vulnerability I do not. But the tight line of his jaw and his pressed-together lips argue otherwise.

"Where are we?" I whisper as I scoot closer to him, taking comfort from the warmth of his skin even as cold fear washes over me.

"We're in a holding cell. This first floor is the Administrator's business headquarters. The living quarters are upstairs, but we cadets were never allowed up there." His eyes narrow as he studies our guards' backs. "I wouldn't be surprised to find Ford 45 in here with us very soon."

I have to admit, that would be the icing on top of a very bitter cupcake.

"Can you reach the knife in my pocket?" Trigger whispers, twisting to give me access.

I shake my head. "They took it while you were unconscious."

Trigger mumbles several angry words I've never heard before.

Several minutes later, I hear footsteps descending a set of stairs. A young woman appears outside our cell, holding a tray full of food. Several hunks of cheese are surrounded by a ring of thin crackers and accompanied by a knife. I have no idea what the smooth brown lumps drizzled in various glazes and frostings are. But they smell amazing.

"The chef prepared way too much for the party," the young woman says, holding the tray out to Gladius and Pike without even a glance at me or Trigger. The name embroidered over her chest is Aida 22. Her name and her familiar face tell me she's a member of the Service Industry division, from a class that graduated several years ago. "Please help yourselves!"

The soldiers glance at each other in obvious hesitation, then Pike speaks for them both. "We couldn't. It's against—"

"The Administrator doesn't tolerate waste." Aida smiles and sets the entire tray on a small table against the wall, only the edge of which is visible from my vantage point. A moment later her steps ascend an unseen staircase.

"Should we?" Pike eyes the tray.

Gladius shrugs. "The Administrator doesn't tolerate waste. I think we *have* to." He uses the small knife to slice a bit of cheese from one of the blocks, then stuffs it into his mouth.

Pike picks up one of the smooth brown lumps and bites off half of it. The inside is gooey, and what looks like a strand of caramel dangles from his lower lip. He groans as he chews. "You *have* to try the chocolates."

Chocolates? I know chocolate as a flavor of cake or frosting, and on cold winter afternoons, when our class has attained victory on field day, as a flavor of warm milk. But I've never heard the word *chocolate* used as a noun.

I turn to Trigger, expecting to see my confusion mirrored on his features, but he's staring at our guards and their food so intently I can practically hear the gears grinding in his head, powering thoughts and ideas I can't even begin to imagine.

"What's a party?" I ask.

Trigger glances at me in obvious surprise. "It's an event where people eat, drink, and play games."

"Like field day?"

"No. It's not athletic. It's more . . . social."

I frown, trying to understand. "To what purpose?"

"To no purpose. It's . . . celebratory. I think. But then I also thought it was an archaic tradition long out of practice. Like celebrating the anniversary of one's birth."

The idea does seem lavish and excessive. And evidently wasteful. People standing around eating and drinking outside of the prescribed mealtime? And playing games for no reason, on a non-recreation day? What for?

But before I can press Trigger for more information, he stands and walks toward the hall.

Pike steps into the doorway, still chewing a gooey brown mouthful. "Stop," he orders. "Sit down."

"I need to use the restroom," Trigger says.

"You'll have to wait." Gladius gestures toward the bench with a sesame-seed-sprinkled cracker in one hand.

"Either take me to the bathroom or get ready to clean up the mess."

Gladius groans and stuffs the cracker into his mouth. Then he grabs Trigger's arm and pulls him down the narrow hallway. I hear a soft snap as his bindings are cut free. A door closes softly and the soldier growls for him to hurry up.

When the door opens again, Trigger's hands are rebound with the soft zip of plastic restraints.

On his way back, while Pike chews another chunk of chocolate, Trigger trips over his own foot and bumps into the tray of food. Gladius yells at him for being clumsy, then shoves him into the cell. When Trigger sits next to me on the bench again, he's wearing an odd smile. His arm brushes mine once, then once again, and I realize he's doing something behind his back.

I lift one eyebrow at him in silent question, and he twists away from me to give me a view of the cheese knife he's using to saw through the plastic zip tie binding his wrists.

My eyes widen. Then I realize my reaction could give him

away, so I rein in my surprise and ecstatic bolt of hope. Not that it matters. Gladius and Pike are still bent over the tray trying one tiny, extravagant morsel at a time.

Trigger works quickly, but the angle is difficult and the cheese knife isn't very sharp, so it takes him several minutes to cut through the plastic. When he's done, he glances at our distracted guards, and when he's sure they're not watching he turns and is able to swiftly cut through my binding in a single firm stroke, since he is no longer limited by his own restraints.

"Keep your hands behind your back," he whispers. "And get ready to run."

Nerves crawl in my belly like an army of ants. But I am ready.

Trigger tenses for a moment with his eyes closed, and I wonder if he's visualizing what he's about to do. Then, in a sudden burst of motion, he explodes off the bench and races across the cell.

Pike looks up as Trigger steps into the hall, cheese knife in hand. Before he can do more than stare in shock Trigger swipes his knife across the inside of the soldier's right elbow, severing the most prominent tendon. I gasp as blood arcs across the floor. Pike screams and slaps his left hand over the gushing, flopping ruin of his right arm.

Trigger grabs the pistol left vulnerable on the injured soldier's right hip and aims it at Gladius, who is frozen in mid-bite. "Drop your gun and kick it toward me."

"You know I can't do that," Gladius insists while Pike whimpers and bleeds a couple feet away.

"Drop the gun and you'll live. Refuse and I'll put a bullet through your forehead."

For one long moment, Gladius stares at Trigger, sizing him up. Does he know Trigger 17 is a member of the Special Forces unit? That he is the best in his class? That he is perfectly capable of carrying out his threat?

Trigger's grip tightens on Pike's pistol. Gladius flinches. "Okay!" The soldier slowly removes his gun from its holster and bends to set it on the ground. He kicks it and the weapon slides across the floor with a clatter, right past Trigger and into the cell where I'm still standing, transfixed.

I glance at it. Should I pick it up? My finger is surely capable of pulling the firing mechanism—the trigger—but is my heart? The soldiers are only doing their job. On a day when so many lives have already been ended, could I possibly take another one?

"You are an embarrassment to your unit." Trigger lowers his aim and fires. The sound is little more than a soft *thwup*, yet I jump. Gladius howls in pain and falls to the floor. Blood pours from a hole in his thigh. "But you'll live," Trigger promises. Then he slams the butt of his stolen gun into the wounded soldier's head.

Gladius goes limp on the floor, still bleeding and now unconscious. One second and another blow to the head later, Pike is also out cold, his bloody right arm flopped on the floor beside him.

Stunned, I can only stare at them both, my hands limp at my sides. I've never seen so much blood. I've never witnessed

199

an injury worse than Violet's soccer concussion. I've never even seen anyone in true pain. But Trigger never hesitated to inflict any of that.

He could just as easily have killed both men.

Why would Lakeview make inferior soldiers like Gladius and Pike, when they could have made more like Trigger?

"Come on!" Trigger waves me out of the room, and I follow him into the hall on shaky legs. We head for the door into the parking lot, but it opens before we get to it, and more soldiers pour into the building, evidently having been alerted by Pike's screams.

"Stop!" they yell as we spin and run back the other way. We pass the open cell and the unconscious guards, then race toward a set of stairs leading to the second floor.

Something whizzes past my head and thunks into the wall, and I stop, staring in shock at a bullet embedded just an inch to the left of my head.

"No!" one of the soldiers shouts behind us. "Ford 45 wants them alive!"

"Go." Trigger pushes me up the next step and I'm running again. "I'll take care of them, then catch up with you."

Before I can argue, he turns and runs toward three soldiers, wielding both the cheese knife and the stolen pistol. I watch long enough to see that they are no match for his training, then I race up the stairs.

The second-floor landing empties into a wide hallway carpeted in a bright red length of rug. Several closed doors line both sides of the hall. I try knobs indiscriminately, but none of them open, and I know better than to stick my wrist beneath the scanners built into the wall beside them.

At the end of the hall there is a door with no scanner and no keyhole. I race toward it and twist the knob, then burst into the largest closet I've ever seen in my life. The room is lined with metal rods, from which hang coats in every color and material imaginable.

I close the door at my back, then stare in fascination at feathers, fur, leather, and some kind of oddly dyed reptile skin. I reach out to run my hand over the fabric, and it is bumpier than I imagined. Yet somehow also smooth. The coat is long enough to reach my knees, with shiny, oversize black buttons, and there's no name embroidered over the left side.

Each of the hangers is labeled with a handwritten tag, but I don't recognize any of the names. As I reach for the nearest tag, puzzled by a name I have no association for, I hear a soft thump from farther into the closet, behind a rack of coats.

"Shit," a male voice mutters.

I'm not familiar with the word, but it seems to mean "ouch."

I stand rooted to the carpet, my heart pounding violently beneath my breastbone. I don't know if I should run and risk being caught by the soldiers or stay and risk being caught by whoever's behind those coats.

Before I can decide, a boy about my age steps around the end of a rack of coats, wearing the strangest suit I've ever seen.

His eyes widen. His mouth falls open. Then he smiles. "Hey, Waverly. What are you doing here?"

SEVENTEEN

"I thought you couldn't come tonight," the strangely dressed boy says.

"I . . . um . . ." I have no idea what to say. He isn't on the run like Trigger and Wexler, nor trying to arrest me like the soldiers are. Which means he has no reason to say anything to me, beyond telling me that my work honors us all. Not that I would know how to respond. I can't tell for sure from how he's dressed what bureau he belongs to.

He's obviously mistaken me for one of my identicals, and the moment I realize that, a fresh ache seizes hold of my chest. Waverly, whoever she was, is now dead. Because she looked like me.

Yet the boy doesn't seem to know that.

How could he recognize my face yet not know that it isn't supposed to exist anymore? There was a citywide bulletin about the recall. Little else will be discussed among the various bureaus for months. Maybe for years.

I glance over my shoulder at the door to the hall. This strange reprieve can't possibly last long. Any minute Trigger will burst into the room looking for me. Or, if he's lost the fight, the soldiers will come to drag me away.

"Waverly?" the boy repeats. And even though he seems concerned about the girl he thinks I am, he hasn't come to the obvious conclusion—mistaken identity—despite the name embroidered on my borrowed jacket.

What union would a girl named Waverly belong to? I can't place the name, but that's not particularly unusual. I don't know all five thousand female trade labor names. But what bewilders me even more is how Waverly, regardless of what union she belongs to, could possibly know this unfamiliar, oddly dressed boy. She shouldn't know *any* boys, other than those in our bureau, and none of the trade labor boys anywhere near my age bear this brown-eyed, fair-skinned, freckle-free, straight-nosed face.

Yet the boy's gaze travels over me with a familiar manner that sets off alarms in my head. No boy other than Trigger 17 has ever looked at me like that. As if he finds pleasure in the view alone, beyond what service I have to offer the city. But this boy isn't looking at me. He's looking at the poor, doomed Waverly.

Have she and he broken the same rules Trigger and I broke?

My heart beats harder at that thought. Maybe I'm not

the *only* anomaly. Maybe this Waverly and I share the same genetic flaws.

However, that doesn't fit with what Wexler 42 told me about the origin of my genome. Could he have been lying? He betrayed Trigger and me to aid his own escape. A man with that little honor could certainly have been lying about everything he told us.

I don't know what to think. Who to believe. How to respond to this unfamiliar boy who seems to think I should know who he is.

Finally, his gaze snags on the name embroidered low on my left shoulder. "Violet," he reads, and his brows dip in confusion. "Where on earth did you get that uniform?"

That's not what I expected him to ask. Why would he assume the uniform doesn't belong to me, rather than assuming he's mistaken Violet 16 for Waverly 16?

My answer is the same either way. "I stole it."

His laugh is loud and joy-filled, as if I've just told him the funniest joke ever. As if he's not afraid of being caught in the closet with a girl he shouldn't even be speaking to. A girl who should be dead. "If only the world could see you now," he says. "How the hell did you plan to sneak into Seren's birthday party in a laborer's uniform?"

Seren? I don't know that name either. But with the mention of a birthday, suddenly I understand. It's just like Trigger said. Like I learned about once in history. Someone's—Seren's—birth is being celebrated in the archaic tradition, presumably with the ceremonial presentation of a cake lit on fire.

The bygone festival is a celebration of excess and waste all squandered on a single person. It fell out of fashion long ago, when technological advancements allowed the production of people en masse, with much greater efficiency.

So who could this Seren be, and why is his birth being celebrated?

Why did he *have* a birth? Was he not removed from incubation on the same day as everyone else in his division?

Is this the party Aida 22 was referring to?

"Waverly?" The boy is frowning now. He looks worried by my silence. But I can hardly focus on that, because I'm still puzzling over his clothes. He's not wearing a uniform. He's wearing a *suit*. Like members of the Management Bureau wear—except rather than Management-black, this boy's pants and jacket are a dignified shade of gray. His lapels are shiny, a subtle yet extravagant detail I've never seen before, and the pressed, button-down shirt beneath his jacket is a much paler shade of the same color.

Why is he wearing the wrong colors? Why is there no name tag pinned to his jacket? Why is he talking to me as if we know each other? As if there is no shame and no risk involved in speaking so casually to a member of another bureau?

Even Trigger 17, with his bold mannerisms in private, treats his infractions with the gravity they merit. But this boy is cavalier with his audacity. No citizen of Lakeview would . . .

My eyes widen as I take in his strange clothes and fearless curiosity, and suddenly I understand.

This boy is not a citizen of Lakeview.

If our Administrator sends delegations to other cities, might it not be possible that other cities would send delegations into Lakeview? Could this boy be in Lakeview on a diplomatic mission? Could this birthday party somehow be part of the diplomacy?

The only part of that theory that doesn't fit is Waverly. How would a diplomat from another city know a sixteen-year-old trade laborer from Lakeview?

He wouldn't. So how . . . ?

And with a sudden jarring leap of intuition, I understand. This boy with odd mannerisms and a dangerously audacious speech pattern hasn't mistaken me for another trade laborer. Waverly is the identical Wexler 42 accidentally sent to another city to fulfill his "special order."

Waverly isn't dead. She's the girl I was meant to be. Hers is the life I was meant to live.

I stagger backward. The understanding that I've just come face to face with my diverted destiny—with what should have been—is enough to rock me off the foundation of my own existence.

If not for the mix-up, I would know this boy. I might wear the strange clothes that are evidently standard in his city. I might not have my name embroidered on all my jackets and aprons, though I can't really make sense of that, because how would anyone know who I was if not for the embroidery?

If not for the mix-up, I might not be a trade laborer.

That idea shakes me like a mental aftershock. I've never

thought about doing anything other than growing hydroponic vegetables. I've never *wanted* to do anything other than grow hydroponic vegetables.

If I hadn't been incubated here in Lakeview as a member of the hydroponic gardening union, I would never have met Poppy. Or Trigger 17.

I would not be who I am now had that mistake not been made.

"What's wrong?" the boy asks, and I realize my eyes have filled with tears. The only identical I have left is Waverly, wherever she is, and this boy believes I am her. That's why he hasn't raised an alarm and given me up to the soldiers.

"Is this about the uniform?" His confusion clears as he decides to believe his own theory about my tears. Before I can figure out how to answer, he ducks around a rack of strange and exotic outerwear. Mystified, I follow him to see that the coat closet is actually much bigger than I'd assumed. It's bigger than my dorm room.

Behind the racks of coats, I find the boy kneeling in front of a trunk—one of dozens lined up around the perimeter of the room. "Margo always brings a spare dress. She can never make up her mind until she sees what everyone else is wearing. Don't tell her I said this, but I think you'll look even better in this one than she does."

He stands holding a garment unlike anything I've ever seen. Rather than the knee-length narrow Management-style skirt I am expecting, the dress he holds out to me is the color of a ripe peach, its long, pleated skirt made of a

207

strange smooth, shiny material. It's sleeveless, and the bodice is trimmed with hundreds of small crystals that reflect the overhead lights back at me like a thousand tiny suns.

I've never seen anything so beautiful. Or so pointlessly extravagant. What kind of recreation could require such a garment? Why would the laborers in the tailor union even have occasion to produce such a thing?

"Oh, and look. There's a jeweled cuff that goes with it too." The boy pushes the dress and cuff at me, brown eyes flashing with satisfaction over his find, and I wish I knew his name so I could politely refuse what he obviously intends as a favor.

I'm supposed to be hiding, and no one wearing such a lavish arrangement of fabric and crystals could possibly blend into a crowd or fit into a tight space.

Unless . . .

"Is this what everyone is wearing? At the party?" The word feels strange on my tongue. The question feels even stranger. But if all the girls at this diplomatic event are wearing the same ridiculous dress, maybe the soldiers won't bother to look at their faces. They'll never expect to find me in anything other than the trade labor athletic uniform I was arrested in.

He laughs again. "Wouldn't that give Margo a fit! Can you imagine two girls wearing the same dress?" His eyes flash with mischievous mirth, and he leans closer, as if he's about to tell me a secret. "The power of their fury and humiliation would cause a planetary collapse." Suddenly his grin widens. "That would make the *best* prank. If you could bribe Margo's seamstress to make you a dress identical to whatever she'll be wearing next, then show up at the event in it before she does! She would have a *total* meltdown! They'd be talking about it for years!"

My confusion leaves only one thing clear: I will not blend in wearing that dress. Not even with the other party attendees.

"I've found what I came for." He holds up a skinny metal bottle with a screw-on lid, then slides it into his jacket pocket. "Hurry up and change. You've already missed half the party."

I accept the dress and the cuff, because I have no other choice. If I refuse he'll realize I'm not Waverly. And maybe if he can mistake me for my identical, so will everyone else at this party.

He goes behind a rack of coats to give me privacy, and as I step out of my shoes, a bolt of fear spears me.

What happened to Trigger? Has he been captured? What will they do to him? I can only imagine that the punishment for trying to help me escape will be much more severe than simply losing a braid.

I drop Violet's jacket onto the floor, and the sight of it lying there, stolen and discarded, makes me inexplicably sad.

"My sister's going to have an *aneurism* when she sees you in her dress," the boy calls through the rack of coats between us.

My hands freeze, my shirt only halfway over my head. "Your sister?"

How can a boy have a sister? In Lakeview, that term applies

209

to one's genetic identicals. The archaic definition refers to genetic siblings, which could be of different genders, but that concept hasn't had relevance in centuries.

Evidently his native city uses the term as a colloquialism.

It's never occurred to me before that other cities could be so different from Lakeview. But as I step out of my pants, I realize I'm not truly surprised. I've known my whole life that Lakeview is the greatest, strongest, most efficient and well-run city in the world, and now I understand why. The others indulge in wasteful, frivolous practices and events, all of which no doubt take time and resources away from their primary purpose: the effective function of the city itself, for the good of all its citizens.

Only once I'm wearing a dress belonging to a girl I've never met do I realize how unprepared I am for the charade I'm about to attempt. I don't know what city this boy and his "sister" are from. I know nothing of its culture, beyond an overview of their wasteful practices. I don't know the people who will be at this party. I don't even know this boy's name, and I can't ask him without exposing my ignorance.

"Are you ready?" he calls.

"I'm dressed," I reply, hoping he won't notice that I haven't actually answered the question.

He steps around the rack of coats, and when he sees me his eyebrows shoot halfway up his forehead. He seems to have run out of words. "Um . . . that dress is a perfect fit. Margo's going to kill us both."

I stare down at the dress, disoriented by the sight of myself, but he seems pleased with the look.

"What are the chances"—he kneels in front of the open trunk again—"that you and Margo wear the same size shoe?" He stands again with the footwear equivalent of the dress I'm wearing—a gem-studded pair of shoes made of straps that appear to be mounted on four-inch stilts.

"Are you sure those are shoes?" I ask, and he laughs as he holds them out to me.

"Right? I don't see how you girls walk in those." Yet he seems to expect me to do exactly that.

I prop myself against the wall with one hand while I step one at a time into the glittery, strappy footwear, and when I stand again, wobbling, I wonder why I even bothered. My skirt covers them entirely.

Either they're a size too small or they were designed to double as instruments of torture.

I plan to ditch the shoes at the earliest opportunity.

The boy waves me forward, and I follow him around the rack of coats toward the exit. He pulls the door open and gestures for me to precede him into the hall, smiling, but I've forgotten how to move.

Standing in the doorway, his dark eyes wide with shock, his hand still reaching for the doorknob the boy has unwittingly pulled out of his reach, is Trigger 17.

EIGHTEEN

"Trigger!" There's a spot of blood on his collar and his knuckles are bruised, but as far as I can see he's alive and unharmed. I have no idea how many soldiers he disabled—or killed?—but I'm so relieved to see him in one piece that for a moment I forget that in the few minutes since we parted ways I've been transformed into the princess from a primary dorm nanny's fanciful bedtime story.

His gaze travels over my borrowed dress and his surprise melts into a frown. "What are you wearing?" He hasn't yet glanced at the boy still holding the door open, but I can tell from the tension in his arms and the tight line of his jaw that he's already assessed the potential threat and is ready to dispatch it.

"It's my sister's dress," the boy says, and Trigger's hard gaze finally fully lands on him.

"Who are you?" Trigger's voice sounds deeper than I've ever heard it. The sound gives me chills.

The boy's brows rise, as if he's startled to have heard Trigger speak. But then he regroups with a determined smile. "I am Hennessy Chapman."

He has *two* names? I try not to let my surprise show. What use has a person for two names? What division would a boy named Hennessy Chapman belong to? And what is his number? How are we supposed to know what class he belongs to if we don't know his age?

"You're Waverly's new man?" he continues, and Trigger's frown deepens. "Her new security, I mean." The boy's face flushes slightly, as if he's just embarrassed himself, but I don't really understand how. Yet I understand enough to seize the opportunity.

"Yes." I nod emphatically, eyeing Trigger, silently begging him to play along because I see no other choice at the moment. "He's my new security."

Comprehension washes over Trigger's face; then his expression goes completely blank. He takes a formal step back from us and clasps his wrists at his back, and though he seems to be staring at nothing, I know he's seeing everything.

He was made to play this role.

"This is Trigger 17," I say. There's no sense lying about his name. It's embroidered over the left side of his uniform jacket.

The boy throws his head back and laughs. "This is unbelievable, Waverly!" he says, and I can't help but agree. "The

213

costumes look so authentic! Your seamstress must have . . ." He shakes his head briefly, as if to clear it of cobwebs. "Wait, you said you stole them, right?"

Seamstress? Costumes? Like Wexler's, his vocabulary leaves me mystified.

"I'm glad you brought him, for your own safety," Hennessy Chapman says. "But does he have to come into the party with you? Most of the personal staff members are waiting at the wall—"

"My orders are to stay with her," Trigger insists, and I glance at him in relief.

"Yes, I need him," I say, and suddenly I'm blushing from the kernel of truth in this lie I'm telling.

"Of course," the boy concedes with an almost formal nod. Then he takes my arm and bends his around it in an awkward interlocking motion.

When we step out of the closet, I notice for the first time, now that I'm not running for my life, how thick and plush the carpet in the hallway is. The walls are lined with some kind of silky fabric, which has an elaborate design stitched in a subtle gold color, just a shade lighter than the material itself.

I let Hennessy Chapman escort me down the strange hallway and around a corner, wishing desperately for a chance to explain to Trigger what he's missed. And to apologize for the role I've unintentionally stuck him in. But he follows several steps behind us, just like the Administrator's private security, and I wonder what Waverly has done to merit her own guard. She's only sixteen. What could she possibly have accomplished in such a short life? Maybe she *is* being trained for something special. . . .

I understand nothing about whatever city Waverly and Hennessy Chapman come from, or about the party I'm about to walk into, or about the girl I'm supposed to be.

They're going to know I'm a fraud.

I must have tensed or done something else to betray my fear, because Hennessy Chapman pats my hand, sandwiching it between his arm and his fingers, and the gesture is obviously intended to be comforting. But in my entire life, Trigger 17 is the only other boy I've touched, and I would have been happy for that to remain true. I wish my arm were tucked into his right now. I wish he were close at my side rather than at my back.

"I can't believe you made it," Hennessy Chapman says as I fight for balance, walking on stilts in the thick carpeting. "I thought they'd have you on total lockdown."

Lockdown? Has my secret identical found as much trouble in her city as I've found in mine?

Trying to piece together information about the girl I'm pretending to be from the fragmented bits that fall from her friend's mouth is both frustrating and terrifying. One wrong word could expose me. But silence when she would have spoken up could expose me too.

I am paralyzed by indecision.

"But I wish you'd told me you were coming," he continues.

"I would have left one of my own men to escort you in. Or I could have brought your trunk with me so you'd have your own clothes to wear."

"Hindsight," I say with a shrug, and to my relief he seems to accept that as an answer.

Hennessy Chapman stops in front of a heavy set of double doors, each intricately carved into four quadrants of a curving design. He lets go of my arm, and I sway a little on my stilts. "I can't wait to see their faces," he says as he throws the doors open with a soft grunt.

Music and aroma and voices wash over me and I stumble backward, stunned. One of Waverly's stupid spiky heels wobbles beneath me, and only my fresh grip on my escort's arm keeps me upright.

"You okay?" he whispers.

I nod as I stare into the huge room, but I don't understand what I'm seeing. There's too much to process at once. There are so many tables full of foods I've never seen before. So much elaborate furnishing. So much light glittering on so many brightly clad bodies. I am overwhelmed by the sights, sounds, and scents.

Dozens of girls and boys around my age lounge on clusters of plushy cushioned, elaborately carved furniture, chatting in groups of three or four. Several dozen more bob and move in time to music blaring from two huge boxes in one corner.

The boys are dressed in Management-style suits, but like Hennessy Chapman they wear different muted shades of blue, gray, or brown. The girls all wear lavish dresses in every conceivable color and style, and—Hennessy Chapman was right—no two are alike. As they move with the beat, paired with boys, they look like exotic flowers floating around the room on a breeze no one can see.

Hennessy Chapman smiles at me. Then he turns back to the room. "Ladies and gentlemen, look who I found!"

Conversations end. The rhythmic bobbing stops. Everyone stares.

Goose bumps pop up all over my skin, and I feel horribly exposed. Paralyzed by the attention. For my entire life, the fewer eyes that have lingered on me, the safer I've felt. Yet suddenly no one seems to be looking at anyone or anything else.

This is the opposite of hiding.

My chest locks around the breath trapped within it, and my throat aches with the effort of dragging in a fresh one.

I am going to die. This is the beginning of the end. Yet on the edges of that thought, as my gaze falls upon wonder after wonder, I realize I am glad—since I am definitely moments from being caught—to have seen such an extraordinary display before I die.

Yes, this party is exorbitantly extravagant and unforgivably wasteful, and terrifyingly . . . conspicuous. But it's also the most *beautiful* thing I've ever seen. All the colors are bright. All the textures are soft, shiny, or glittery. And the food . . .

My mouth waters so insistently that I have to swallow to

keep from drooling. I've never smelled so many tantalizing scents, and the amazing part is that I recognize most of them!

For years I've grown food I never saw served. I've always assumed the fruits and vegetables and herbs and spices that never made their way onto my dinner tray were served to the adult residents of Lakeview. That after graduation I'd finally be allowed to sample the full selection of produce I've been growing my whole life.

Now that will never happen.

But at least I'll have had this glimpse of tiny slices of meat I can't identify, marinated in tantalizing combinations of spices I've hand-picked from their stems. Of vegetables blended together and served on delicate little crackers made from wheats and grains I always found to be more trouble to grow than they were worth, when they were only used in the coarse breads we're served in the cafeteria.

And if I step into this huge room and face this crowd of gawkers, I might even get to taste these delicacies before the soldiers descend on me and drag me away.

Finally, after several of the longest seconds of my life, a girl stands from a low upholstered stool and holds her arms out for me. "Waverly!" Her hair is blond and too long to be practical, and her bright white smile seems to welcome me. Her lilac dress swishes around her feet as she crosses the room toward me. "I'm so glad you could make it!"

As she comes closer, I notice something strange about her face. While she looked beautiful at a distance and still does, in an odd way, up close, it's now easy to see that her face has been . . . *painted*. Her lips and her eyes appear to have been drawn on.

As strange as this custom seems at first, given the elaborate dresses and ridiculous shoes, maybe the face paint shouldn't come as much of a surprise.

Hennessy Chapman lets me go as the painted girl pulls me into an embrace. Her warm breath brushes my left ear. "What in the *living hell* are you doing in my dress, you thieving bitch?"

Margo. It has to be. I don't understand half of what she's said, but I can hear the fury in her voice.

Before I have a chance to tell her that her brother insisted I wear the dress, she's holding me at arm's length, beaming at me as if she's never been happier to see anyone in her life.

The sudden change makes my head spin.

"Hennessy, what the hell?" she demands softly as she turns from me to take his arm. And now I feel like an even bigger fool. She's only using the first of his two names. And he's addressed her by a single name.

Does that mean Waverly has a second name as well?

"Don't be mad," he insists. "Waverly had to sneak into the city in disguise, and she couldn't exactly bring a trunk, could she?"

"So you gave her my dress?" Margo hisses softly as others stand and head our way.

"Hennessy meant no harm," I assure her in a soft voice, since they're both whispering. "He thought he'd be doing you a favor, because it looks so much better on me."

Hennessy's laughter echoes across the room. Margo's sharp inhalation and her shocked-wide eyes are my only clue that I've just said something wrong.

Her brows lower and her brown eyes darken with fury. "You brash little slut!" she hisses, too low for anyone else to hear.

I have no idea what she's just called me, but I've obviously made things worse.

"It's only a loan," I assure her just as softly, but her eyes narrow when she turns back to me. "I fully intend to return the dress."

"As if I can ever wear it now that everyone's seen it on you."

I'm not sure what she means, but there's no time to ask for a clarification of something Waverly would probably understand, because suddenly we are surrounded by other people. Boys and girls call out my clone's name and fuss over my dress, and as I try to pretend I know them all without using any names, I finally notice the most extraordinary part of this odd wonderland.

It isn't just the dresses that are one of a kind—it's the people too. I see a dizzying array of heights and a dazzling spectrum of skin tones, and no two sets of features look alike. There are no names or numbers embroidered on their clothing.

These people are—all of them—individuals. Which must mean that in her city, Waverly doesn't stand out for being unique.

I can hardly wrap my mind around that concept. People engineered one at a time. No two alike. The process must be incredibly labor-intensive. Their city must have hundreds of geneticists. Or *thousands*! But why would any city persist with such an inefficient process?

I glance around the room again and notice that though the girls each have a distinctly different set of features, they all seem to share that same painted quality Margo has. Their lashes are all dark and thick, and something bright and glittery has been smeared into the creases of their eyelids, which makes their eyes look quite prominent and bright.

Their skin is universally smooth and flawless, and their lips seem just a little too plump and symmetrical. As if this collection of individuals, each determined to wear unique clothing, all secretly want to look alike.

"Waverly!" A boy in a dark green suit brushes one hand down my arm. "Did you really sneak into Lakeview disguised as a common laborer? That is *so* badass!"

A common laborer? Is there an uncommon variety?

"As if anyone would believe she was a clone," one of the girls says to the boy next to her, eyes sparkling as if she's just heard the *best* joke. "Can you imagine hundreds of Waverlys walking around with calluses on their hands and dirt under their nails?"

Try thousands.

But that thought makes my eyes water. I cannot afford to cry here. So I push my grief back and try not to hate all these people who think the sisters I've just lost are nothing more than a joke.

That's why they're falling for my act. It's not that I'm good at pretending to be their friend. It's that they have no choice but to believe what their eyes are telling them unless I make a *huge* mistake, because they don't know there's any other option.

They think that Waverly, like all of them, is one of a kind.

I get lost in the greetings, pointless chatter, and unintelligible jokes. Half of their vocabulary is indecipherable, which is just as well, because nothing I hear seems to truly mean anything anyway.

Finally, just when the noise and confusion threaten to overwhelm me completely, a hand slides into mine and I exhale in relief. Then I look up and disappointment washes over me when I realize that the hand belongs to Hennessy.

Trigger has retreated to the edge of the room, where a few other personal guards stand. They are all enough older than us that I don't recognize their faces. However, I notice that two of them are identical.

So the partygoers are one of a kind, but the private guards are not?

I don't understand the strange new world I've stepped into. But suddenly I am grateful for Hennessy's hand and his apparent willingness to let me hold on to it.

Finally the crowd around us starts to disperse. Couples return to the center of the room to "dance" to the music. Groups return to their seated conversations centered around topics I can't even begin to understand. But one boy is still making his way across the floor toward Hennessy and me, carrying two tall, delicate stemmed glasses. His suit is the color of the night sky, the darkest blue I can imagine, with shiny black lapels and matching shoes.

"Waverly!" He leans forward to kiss me on the cheek, and I suck in a surprised breath. "I hear you pulled out all the stops to sneak into the enigmatic Lakeview compound, just to come wish me a happy birthday!"

Compound?

I give him a smile. "Happy birthday, Seren." I am so thrilled and relieved to have figured out his name that I don't even hesitate to speak to him, despite a lifetime of training to the contrary.

Smiling, he holds one empty stemmed glass into the stream of a pale golden liquid flowing from the fountain in the center of the nearest table full of food. The liquid fizzes in the glass. He hands it to me, and though I know he intends for me to drink, I can do nothing but stare at his right wrist, where it is extended from the cuff of his shirt.

He has no bar code.

How can he function in life with no bar code? How can he sign in for an appointment or check out recreational equipment without one? How can he get a lunch tray or be issued a fresh set of clothes? How does he gain access to his tablet? How will he someday start a CitiCar?

Surely in his native city not every meal is served on crystal plates, from tables piled high with food. Surely not every drink pours from a fountain.

I glance around the room again as I slowly lift the glass to my mouth. The boys' wrists are covered by their shirt cuffs and jacket sleeves, but most of the girls' wrists are exposed by sleeveless dresses. Not one of them has a bar code.

Who *are* these people?

"Waverly?" Hennessy has noticed me hesitating with the glass inches from my lips. "Are you okay?"

"I'm fine. Thank you," I say, but the common courtesy seems to confuse him even more. So I drink, and the bubbles pop in my nose and mouth.

I laugh at the strange sensation. Then I take a longer sip.

"Your favorite, right?" Seren says as he fills his own glass.

I can only nod. I have no idea what Waverly's favorite is, or what I'm drinking. It's sweet, yet the undertone is a bit bitter. It's not unpleasant, but it will take some getting used to. The best part is the bubbles.

As I lift the glass for another sip, the jeweled cuff slides up my arm, revealing a thin slice of my bar code. Terrified that I've exposed myself, I hastily transfer the glass into my opposite hand and shake the cuff down to cover my right wrist. Just in case, I keep that arm pressed against my side.

As I stare off into the room, glancing from face to face—dizzied by the variety of features and the lack of any unifying color, clothing, or mark—the reality of this strange world finally hits me.

These people belong to no bureau. They aren't gardeners, soldiers, seamstresses, or cooks. In fact, they seem to serve no purpose whatsoever.

Was I, like Waverly's friends, created to serve no purpose? For no other reason than to eat extravagant food while we say nice things to one another aloud, then whisper angrily into one another's ears?

If that is so, why was I ever given life?

Why were any of the partygoers in this room ever designed in the first place?

NINETEEN

"What is this?" I hold my glass up for Hennessy to see when we're alone in the crowd again.

"The champagne? I don't know what vintage Seren is serving, but knowing the Administrator, it's expensive."

I have no idea what champagne is, but I'm even more confused by what the Administrator might have to do with a party thrown for a boy—an *individual*—from another city. At first I assumed that she was simply hosting a diplomatic event, but the guests are all my age, and they seem to represent no one but themselves.

While Hennessy fills his own glass, Margo returns with another girl and they each take one of my arms. I feel as trapped as I was in my cell at the Management Bureau. And a lot less safe.

"Doesn't Waverly look beautiful tonight, Sofia?" Margo says, and relief floods me. Evidently she's no longer angry about the dress.

Then I get a good look at her friend's long dark hair and olive-toned skin. She looks different, with her face painted, but I recognize her anyway.

Sofia is the girl I saw arguing with two soldiers on a sidewalk in the training ward the day several thousand of Trigger's identicals graduated. The bold girl wearing strange clothes, who kept refusing to get into the patrol car.

She didn't even glance at me or my identicals that day. If she'd noticed our faces, Waverly's secret would already have been exposed.

My act wouldn't be working.

"She does look beautiful," Sofia says, squeezing my arm while I try to piece together facts and events that don't seem to fit. I deduce from her resemblance to Seren—how can she look so much like him yet still be a girl?—that she is his "sister." They must share *some* strange genetic connection, but I can't understand how.

"Where did you have that dress made?" she asks. But her too-wide eyes and pursed lips make me think she isn't really interested in the answer. Which is fortunate, because I don't have one.

"I love what you've done with your hair tonight, Waverly," Margo says. "It's so I-don't-give-a-shit. That must feel liberating."

"I . . ." Her statement sounds like a compliment, but it feels like biting into an apple that has gone bad on the inside. Maybe she's still angry after all.

"It's not like she could go get her hair done," Sofia says. "No one would have believed her as a trade laborer when she was sneaking in through the *service* entrance."

"Of course. And I guess that explains this *au naturel* thing you have going on with your face." Margo makes a gesture vaguely encompassing my head, and I can feel my cheeks flame. I don't understand everything they're saying, but I'm clearly being made fun of. I'm the only girl here whose face isn't painted.

"Don't worry about these hyenas." Hennessy plucks his sister's hand from my arm. "They're just jealous because it takes them hours in a salon chair to look half as beautiful as you do when you roll out of bed in the morning."

Salon chair?

"You're laying it on thick this evening, brother," Margo says. But she actually looks a little contrite. I don't think she intended for him to hear her.

"Waverly can handle herself," Sofia adds. "And anyway, we're not throwing any muck she hasn't thrown at us a thousand times."

"Thank you," I whisper to Hennessy as both girls head onto the dance floor, where two boys are obviously waiting for them.

"Are you okay?" he asks, just loudly enough to be heard over the music. "You seem kind of out of it tonight."

My gaze wanders toward Trigger, and I find him watching me. His clenched jaw is the only sign that he's not perfectly happy playing his role while this strange new boy holds my arm and whispers in my ear.

Trigger is clearly as ready to leave this dangerous charade behind as I am now that the novelty has worn off. But I don't know *where* to go. This private party in the Administrator's mansion seems to be the only place in Lakeview that the soldiers won't search for us.

Hennessy is still watching me in concern. "Is this about your parents?"

"Parents?" I want to laugh at the first joke I've been able to clearly recognize all evening, but he beats me to it.

"You know, the tight-fisted bastard and stone-cold bitch who birthed and raised you but forced you to sneak out to attend the party of the year? Or are they dead to you as a result of such brutal social injustice?"

Parents. It's an archaic general descriptor for a set of caregivers, typically a father who physically sired children and a mother who physically incubated and gave birth to them in a messy, bloody, dangerous procedure.

Centuries ago.

When the world was different.

Yet Hennessy isn't laughing anymore. He's using the term as if it has current relevance. As if I came not from an incubator in a lab but from *inside* a *woman*. As if I belong not to a bureau, or a division, or even a city, but to a pair of individuals who conceived me with *bodily fluids*. But that's

229

not possible. That kind of messy genetic transfer isn't done anymore.

Is it?

My head spins as I stare around the room.

Is that how they get so many individuals? Are people in Waverly's city not designed by geneticists and grown in incubators? Are they not cared for by nannies, then dormitory floor conservators? Is Waverly's city populated *entirely* by individuals?

How can they have such advanced food preparation techniques and clothing design and face-enhancing paint yet have mastered so little of the basic technology that keeps a city functioning at maximum capacity and efficiency?

How can they populate their academies, if every citizen requires different considerations and accommodations? If they aren't all designed to specifically fulfill the needs of the city they serve?

Do they serve their city *at all*?

From our basic geography unit, I know approximately where all the neighboring cities are. Mountainside, Riverbend, Oceanbay, Valleybrook. But I don't know which of them is the anomalous metropolis where people are conceived rather than designed and born rather than removed from incubation. Nor do I understand why the Administrator would host a party for the children of such a city.

"Waverly?"

"I'm fine," I assure Hennessy, hoping to rid him of the concern lining his features, which is sure to evolve into suspicion if I keep saying and doing the wrong things.

Something beeps from my left, and I drag my gaze away from Trigger to see that Hennessy has pulled a small tablet from his pocket. A *very* small tablet, no longer than his hand. He taps on an icon, then reads a couple of sentences of a ping someone has sent him.

"My driver says our car is lined up out front with all the others and Margo's trunk is being loaded. We'll be leaving in about ten minutes."

Panic burns like fire surging through my veins. When the guests have all gone, there will be no reason for Waverly to remain. My disguise will expire with this party.

He misinterprets my fear. "You can't send for your car, can you? Because you snuck in. Let me take you and your guard home."

Home. A brand-new fear fires through me. I can't go to Waverly's home, where it will become *immediately* obvious that there are two of us.

Yet I can't stay here either. But if Hennessy's car gets me out of Lakeview . . .

"Yes! Thank you."

He stands and offers me his hand. "Dance with me once, before we go? We can't take pictures, since you're not supposed to be here, but . . ."

I've seen thousands of photographs of plants in every possible stage of growth in class, but I'm not sure how one would "take" a picture, or what that has to do with dancing.

What I *am* sure of is that I don't know how to dance. I can hardly even walk in these shoes. But I take his hand and

231

stand, because I can't imagine he would ask Waverly in the first place if he didn't think she would accept.

If I weren't afraid it would draw even more attention my way, I would just trip and fake a twisted ankle. Or actually twist my ankle. Though that would add an extra layer of difficulty to everything when Trigger and I flee into the wild after the party.

I glance back at him as Hennessy leads me toward the center of the room, and my "private security" is still watching me with his jaw clenched. He doesn't want me to dance with Hennessy. *I* don't want to dance with Hennessy. I take a deep breath, ready to let my insanely high left heel slip out from under me, when suddenly the heavy double doors at the end of the room fly open.

At least two dozen identical soldiers pour inside from the hallway and the music screeches to a halt. Couples go still and groups rise, startled, from clusters of furniture. Shocked silence stretches across the huge room. Everyone stares at the soldiers, waiting for an explanation for the interruption.

The soldiers stare back without breaking their formation or even turning their heads. Their eyes are as wide as their posture is stiff. They look as astonished as I've been since the moment I entered the room.

A man pushes his way between the soldiers, and I suck in a startled breath when I recognize both his face and the name tag pinned to his black suit. Ford 45 scans the sea of faces without settling on any of them. He does not seem surprised that the partygoers are not identicals.

"Please remain calm!" he orders. But every muscle in my body demands that I flee. "These soldiers only need a minute of your time. Then you'll be free to carry on with your"—his disgusted expression roams the room again—"party."

TWENTY

Panic tightens my grip on Hennessy's hand. Trigger steps away from the wall, his hands open at his sides, ready for action, but I subtly wave him back. Ford 45 hasn't noticed us. The last thing we want to do is draw his attention.

The soldiers spread out into a loose formation, and their commander marches through the ranks to stand next to Ford. "I apologize for the interruption," he begins, addressing the crowd. "But—"

"You better have a hell of a lot more than an apology to offer!" Seren strides through the room as if he owns it, Sofia on his heels, and stops just feet from Ford and the commander. "This is my birthday party. You have no business here. Our mother is the Administrator, and she will—"

"Your mother is the one who sent us, sir," the commander

replies, and for a second the room seems to spin around me. "We're here to search for fugitives."

The *Administrator* is a *mother*?

Of every startling bit of information I've puzzled my way through in the past hour, this one is the most difficult to believe. The Administrator isn't from another city, where they don't understand the efficiency and superiority of the mass production of specially designed citizens, each suited to a specific purpose. She is from Lakeview. She is one of us. And like the rest of us, she was once one of many identicals cloned from a single genome.

How could such a woman have given birth? *Why* would she have given birth, when the training center is full of children of every age, learning every conceivable skill to be of service to the city?

With *whom* could she have conceived children?

Suddenly the Administrator's mansion makes a certain kind of stunning sense. It *is* a family home—and the best-kept secret in Lakeview. No wonder Sofia's guards were so eager to get her out of the training ward that day. She and Seren must be confined to the mansion to keep their existence a secret from the rest of the city.

Though Ford 45 obviously already knew about them.

"Are we in danger?" Sofia demands, drawing my attention back to the confrontation between the Administrator's apparent children and the soldiers.

"No," the commander insists, and I wonder whether he's

lying or truly doesn't know how many of his men Trigger has already disabled. "But we're under orders to check every square foot of the mansion."

"Well then, carry on," Seren says. "But make it quick."

The soldiers spread out and begin looking under covered tables and lifting heavy pieces of furniture. I slide behind Hennessy as subtly as I can, trying to keep my face out of their direct line of sight, but several soldiers walk right past me without even a glance.

They don't expect to find the last remaining member of the year-sixteen trade labor division wearing a sparkly dress and dangerous shoes.

However, Trigger is still wearing his cadet uniform with his name embroidered on the front. Unlike Hennessy, the soldiers will not be fooled by his "disguise" if they see him.

"Are they looking for you?" Margo whispers as she steps up to my left side, too close for comfort.

"Of course they're not looking for her!" Hennessy snaps. Then he turns to me, and the doubt in his eyes is as clear as the doubt in his voice. "Right? Your parents wouldn't send the troops after you for sneaking out, would they?"

I shrug, terrified of exposing my ignorance. "They've already walked right past me several times." I have to get Trigger out of here, though. Immediately. "But maybe I should go. I mean, I'm not supposed to be here, and . . ." I shrug, letting them draw their own conclusions.

"And if you get dragged home by the troops again, you'll be grounded for the rest of your life," Hennessy says.

I nod, wondering why Waverly was dragged home by the troops last time.

"Are you sure your new guard won't rat you out?" Margo asks, and I notice that she sounds a little hopeful as she eyes Trigger.

"He's very loyal."

"Well, come on, then." Hennessy grabs my hand. "Let's get out of here."

"I'm not ready to go!" Margo whines as we head toward Trigger, who's still watching us suspiciously from his position against the wall.

"The party's practically over anyway," her brother says with a glance over his shoulder.

"What's going on?" Trigger asks when we're close enough to hear him, his voice soft but distinct.

"The party's over," I tell him, and his gaze drops to my hand, which is enfolded in Hennessy's. "They're going to give us a ride home."

"Home?" Trigger's focus narrows on me, and I can see the unspoken warning in his eyes. But this is our only way out, and with so many soldiers searching the party room, anywhere in the world is preferable to where we are now.

On our way toward the exit, Margo and Sofia hug good-bye, and Hennessy and Seren thump each other on the back, which seems to be the male equivalent of a hug.

I hang back with Trigger, my heart hammering in my ears. How can we get out of the room without drawing attention?

"Where are we going?" he whispers.

"*They're* going to whatever city Waverly lives in. But we could get out of the car in the wild, right? We don't have to go the whole way."

He gives me a slight shake of his head. "We won't make it in the wild without supplies. Not this close to winter. We'll ditch them and their car as soon as we're in this other city and take what we need from there."

Before I can argue or express any doubts—and I have several—Hennessy is waving us forward.

My heart threatens to burst through my rib cage when the soldier stationed at the door tries to stop us from leaving. But before I can panic or Trigger can try to disable him, Seren steps up, toe to toe with the soldier.

"I absolutely draw the line at the harassment of my guests. This is Hennessy and Margo Chapman, and Waverly Whitmore, of Mountainside. They've done nothing wrong, and now they wish to leave. So step the hell back."

The soldier tries to argue, and Seren starts yelling.

"Come on!" Margo grabs my hand and tugs me through the doorway past the guard. Her eyes are bright with excitement at the prospect of an "escape," and my use of her dress seems to have been forgiven.

Hennessy follows us out the door, but I can't breathe until I see Trigger step into the hall behind him, unscathed. The soldier is too busy arguing with the Administrator's son to notice.

"Why are we running?" Hennessy asks as I hobble down

the hall as fast as I can go, trying to keep up with his sister. Who is evidently *truly* his sister.

"Because if he checks our names against the list, he'll figure out that Waverly didn't come in with the rest of us," Margo explains, as if it should be obvious. "But if you *want* her to get taken into custody and delivered to her parents in time to be grounded for the rest of her life, we can go back . . . ?" She slows to a walk and tosses her brother a teasing smile.

"We're *not* going back," Trigger insists, and they both glance at him in surprise. Evidently the personal guard isn't supposed to participate in conversation.

"Agreed," I say, drawing attention away from him.

"Then let's go!" Margo bends to remove her shoes, then takes off at a jog, holding both of the stilt-like death traps in one hand. I follow her lead, and a second later we're racing down the hall in the opposite direction of the back staircase Trigger and I took earlier.

We pass several more doors, then come to a wide, curving staircase overlooking a massive foyer. From this perspective, the Administrator's mansion looks less like a house than a bureau, but as we race down the stairs I understand that in truth, it is both.

On the first floor, Margo shoves her way through a set of glass double doors and we spill out onto a wide front porch edged by a broadly curved set of stone steps. In the circular drive in front of the mansion is a long line of black cars sitting almost bumper to bumper along the cruise strip.

Though I don't know how they can distinguish it from the others, Hennessy and Margo head straight for the second car in line, and when the man in the front seat sees them coming, he gets out to open a back door for them. Margo climbs onto the rear bench seat and scoots to make room. Hennessy gestures for me to go first, so I slide in, and he follows me.

Trigger gets into the front seat without being asked, and the man who held the door open circles the car to sit next to him.

This man—the driver?—holds his wrist beneath a scanner on the dashboard and the engine rumbles to life. I stare at his bar code and understand that even though I don't recognize his genome, he is a clone.

But I have no idea why he is in Hennessy's car or why it needs a driver.

The car parked in front of ours moves forward a couple of feet, and the man sitting in its front seat gives Hennessy's driver a courteous wave.

"Main gate," our driver says when the car prompts him for a destination, and the car gains speed as it rolls forward.

As we're pulling out of the driveway and onto the road, following the cruise strip, I hear a commotion behind us. Adrenaline firing through my veins, I twist in my seat to see soldiers pouring out of the mansion, shouting for the driver to stop the car.

"Keep going," Hennessy demands. "Faster."

"Maximum speed," the driver says, and the car lurches forward, racing down the road at a greater velocity than I've ever imagined. My heart pounds. My body seems stuck to the seat back.

Margo laughs as we leave the soldiers shouting after us.

"Now, *that* is how you make an exit!" Hennessy shouts, his eyes bright with excitement, and I flinch because his mouth is too close to my ear.

Margo turns to me, smiling in the intermittent glow of streetlights as we race past them. "Gotta hand it to you, Waverly. There's never a dull moment when you're involved. Even if you are a thieving bitch."

She's calling me names again, but this time she doesn't seem angry. And I still have no idea how to respond. I glance into the front seat and find Trigger staring out his window, gripping the door handle with white knuckles.

I follow his gaze and find myself as transfixed as he is. The training ward is flying by on our right, and I've never seen it like this before. Though the buildings tower over the ward walls, they don't look as tall from this distance. Most of the academies are dark at this time of night, but the dormitories are towers of light because no one has gone to bed yet except the small children.

But in seconds the training ward is gone.

The administrative ward flies by in a blur of light; then . . . there is nothing but darkness. Empty fields, mown short.

Where's the residential ward? The industrial ward? Where are all the people who live and work in Lakeview after graduation?

How could the city possibly be so small?

A flash of blue catches the corner of my eye and I turn to see a Defense vehicle speeding along behind us, flashing its lights.

"I apologize, sir," the driver says, glancing in the rearview mirror as he begins to slow the vehicle. "But we're being pulled over."

Evidently the soldiers want us to stop the car.

"No!" I grip Hennessy's hand as fear shoots up my spine.

"Ma'am, I have to stop," the driver explains apologetically. "That's the law here, just like it is in your city."

Mountainside. The city my last remaining identical calls home.

"Please." I turn to Hennessy, trying to ignore the look Trigger is giving me from the front seat.

Hennessy looks surprised by both the grip I have on his hand and the desperation in my voice. He glances through the rear window at the car following us. The soldiers turn on their siren, and its wail chases us just as frenetically as the lights.

Hennessy turns back to me, and his eyes light up again at the prospect of defying the soldiers. "Step on it," he says, and before I can ask what that means, the driver responds.

"We're already at maximum automatic speed, sir."

"Then put it in manual."

"Yes, sir." The driver holds his wrist beneath the scanner and the interior of the car glows red as it scans his bar code. "Manual override," he says. Something in the dashboard hums, and as we fly down the road, a panel slides back to reveal a thin leather-wrapped wheel sunken into the dash. The wheel slides forward and the driver grips it. His knee rises into sight from my position in the middle of the backseat; then he stomps on something.

The car shoots forward. He grips the wheel, and when he makes a minor adjustment the car swerves slightly. Our vehicle is no longer being guided by the cruise strips painted on the road. The driver is in total control of the car and everyone in it.

Startled by that realization, I look around for something to hold on to as we pull away from the Defense vehicle. The front gate looms ahead. Behind us the world is awash in bright red and blue.

Trigger grips the door handle on his right. The gate begins to roll closed, no doubt in response to an alert that has gone out.

"Faster!" Hennessy shouts, and Margo squeals with excitement while I squeeze her brother's hand because I have nothing else to hold on to.

The driver stomps harder and the car lurches forward again. The sirens fade into the distance. Our car shoots through the open gate and into the wild.

I am outside Lakeview for the first time in my life. But I don't truly begin to breathe easier until I turn and see that the Defense vehicles—there are three of them now—have stopped at the city limit, evidently the boundary of their authority.

I turn again to see relief shining in Trigger's eyes. I give him a nervous smile, then stare through the windshield in surprise. The cars headlights illuminate the road ahead of us, which is how I can see that though it's paved out here in the wild, probably all the way to the nearest city, there are no more cruise strips.

That's why guests need drivers. There are no CitiCars in the wild.

"Yeah!" Margo throws her fist into the air, and though I'm unfamiliar with the gesture I can feel the celebration in it.

Hennessy squeezes my hand and I look up to find him grinning at me. He and his sister have no idea what they've really done for me and Trigger, but they seem just as pleased with the result as I am. As Trigger is . . .

But Trigger's relief is dampened by an edge of caution in the lines on his forehead. In the hard set of his jaw. His eyes silently remind me that we may be out of Lakeview, but we are not out of the woods. Or rather, we're not yet *in* the woods.

I nod, telling him silently that I remember the plan: Ditch Hennessy and Margo once we're in their city. Steal whatever supplies we can find. Then find a way out of Mountainside.

Where no one will be hunting us.

TWENTY-ONE

I don't realize how tired I am until I catch myself dozing off in the car and suddenly sit straight up. Trigger chuckles softly.

Margo's adrenaline didn't last long, and once we hit the foothills the gentle rocking of the car lulled her right to sleep.

Hennessy held out longer. He wanted to talk, and eventually I pretended to fall asleep so he couldn't ask me any more questions that might expose my ignorance.

Then I actually fell asleep.

I look to my right and find Hennessy snoring softly on the bench seat, his head propped against the window.

Trigger has been awake and on alert the whole time.

"How much farther is it?" I ask the driver.

"Just a few minutes now," he answers just as softly, without taking his focus from the road. "We'll have you home and in bed within half an hour."

If only that were true . . .

"Stop the car!" Trigger says, staring out his window, and the driver jumps, startled.

"Why?"

Trigger turns to me, and his eyes practically glow with excitement in the dim light from the dashboard. "Wild apples," he whispers.

"Stop," I whisper, smiling. "Please."

The driver shrugs, then slows the car to a stop in the middle of the road.

"We'll only be a minute," Trigger says as he pushes his door open.

Crisp, cold air floods the interior of the car, and I hurriedly climb over Margo so I can close the door without waking either her or her brother.

"I saw them in the headlights," Trigger says as he leads me through a patch of crunchy, overgrown grass, his hand warm in mine. Weeds catch on the bottom of my dress and scratch my legs, but I can see where we're headed. Just yards from the car, a cluster of broad trees stand in the moonlight, branches weighed down by round red fruit.

"Spartan apples," I say as we come to a stop beneath the closest tree. "Historically harvested in the fall." But I've only ever seen them in the hydroponic orchard.

"Pick one," Trigger says.

He watches my face as I reach up and touch one of the small, almost perfectly round fruits. Its flesh is rougher than I expected. Its leaves are a bright green, even in the dark.

I give the apple a gentle twist, then a tug. The branch bobs as it pulls free. And I am holding my very first fruit plucked straight from the tree.

I hold it to my nose and inhale. The scent is sweet, with a slight tang. The Spartan is a great apple for juicing. Or for eating right from the core.

I take a bite and my teeth burst through the skin into crisp, sweet flesh. Juice drips down my chin. I laugh out loud.

This apple tastes wild. Like earth and wind, with a wonderful natural sweetness. And though it's red and round like all the others growing in the branches of the same tree, it is subtly different from *all* of them.

"They're still asleep," Trigger whispers as I swallow my first bite.

I glance back at the car to make sure, then I pull Trigger down and kiss him in the moonlight. Under the apple tree. With fresh juice still damp on my lips.

He tastes wild too.

"I don't want to get back in the car," I murmur when that first wild kiss ends.

"I know," he says. "But we have to. You're already shivering."

I hadn't even noticed. But he's right. It's too cold to stay outside without supplies.

"We're almost to Mountainside. We'll take what we need, then find a way back through the gate. We'll be back here before you know it."

"Promise?" I say as we head for the car.

"I swear."

"Hey." Hennessy sits up as I climb back into the backseat, still carrying my apple. "What's wrong?"

"Nothing." I take another bite, then speak around it. "I got hungry."

"That thing's probably dirty," Margo says, pushing tangled hair back from her face.

"Yeah." I smile to myself. "It is."

The car rolls forward again, and the angle of the road steepens sharply. We are driving up the side of the mountain now. Trigger turns in his seat to watch me until Hennessy takes my hand, and for the thousandth time I wonder exactly how close Hennessy and Waverly are. I've already deduced that there are no rules against fraternization in Mountainside, which leaves possibilities well beyond what my limited imagination can come up with.

It's strange and disillusioning to suddenly realize I know very little about the world, and even less about the people in it.

Margo sits straighter when the city comes into view. She stares through the windshield at her home as if the scene means little to her, but it takes every bit of self-control I have not to gasp at the sight.

Mountainside is much bigger than I expected. Much bigger than Lakeview.

From this distance, the buildings don't look as tall as the dormitories or the Workforce Academy at home, but there are many, many more of them. They seem to climb the side of the mountain, which leaves them in plain view over the city walls, and even in the middle of the night about half of them are lit up.

My heart pounds as we approach the gate. None of my identicals ever left Lakeview. I never expected to see anything of the world beyond the walls of the city where I was designed, created, incubated, and raised.

Hennessy's driver rolls the car to a stop at the city gate. The road is so steep that I am forced to lean back in my seat, and the windshield seems to face directly up into the sky. The driver presses a button and his window descends into the car door. A guard leans down so he can see inside the vehicle.

I blink, certain my tired eyes are seeing things that aren't really there.

The guard's uniform reads GLADIUS 28. But that's a Lakeview soldier's name. Does Mountainside use the same names my native city does?

The guard opens his mouth to ask a question, but the words die on his tongue the moment his gaze finds my face. "Ms. Whitmore," he says, clearly surprised. He lifts a tablet and taps a few keys. "I have no record of you leaving the city tonight. . . ."

Hennessy laughs. "Surely that can't be a first for you, soldier. Open the gate and let us through."

Gladius 28 gives him a sharp nod of compliance, then taps something else on his tablet. The gate rolls open smoothly and relatively quickly, and as soon as the opening is wide enough the driver takes us through it.

Just inside the gate, he stops the car and says, "Automatic

engage." The dashboard hums as the steering wheel recedes into its cavity and a panel slides shut over it. "Whitmore estate," the driver says and the car rolls forward again, this time following the cruise strip on the road, which looks just like the ones painted down every road in Lakeview.

Though the sun has been down for hours, the area of Mountainside laid out immediately past the front gate is lit up like broad daylight by pole-mounted light fixtures lining the streets. Tall buildings are crammed close together just feet from the sidewalk, and the grounds seem to be entirely paved. I can't see so much as a blade of grass from my vantage point in the center of the backseat.

Just as I become convinced that Mountainside doesn't have a thing in common with Lakeview, movement catches my eye through Margo's window. I lean around her, and as the car rolls down the street I am surprised to see laborers in familiar brown uniforms sweeping trash down the sidewalks while most residents of Mountainside sleep. The longer I stare out the windows, the more laborers I notice. Six women with identical faces, wearing identical green landscape gardening uniforms, kneel in a flower bed between the street and the sidewalk, planting greenery. Another half-dozen men pull garbage cans to the side of the street from the fronts of various buildings.

But the few citizens I see walking down the sidewalk and frequenting businesses this late at night—those who are out enjoying the late hour rather than working—are individuals. No two of them look alike. No two wear the same clothing.

Our car rolls to a stop, and I glance through the windshield to see that we're sitting in front of a pole suspended vertically over the middle of the street. Hanging from the pole is a single red light. I have to bite my tongue to keep from asking why we're stopped in front of a red light, because I'm sure that's something Waverly would already know.

While the car idles, I look out Hennessy's window and see another group of six landscape gardeners working in the middle of the night, but the timing isn't what makes my eyes widen until they feel as if they will pop out of my skull.

I know those faces.

The gardeners are all girls, and they all have pale curls, narrow-set dark eyes, and long, straight noses. If I were any closer, I know I'd see a sprinkling of freckles across the bridge of their noses.

When the car begins to roll forward again—the red light is now green—we pass closely enough for me to see the name embroidered across the front of one uniform.

AZALEA 19.

I gasp. I *know* those girls. I know their faces, anyway, because I saw them in the Workforce Academy's cafeteria every day for years. They are from the landscape gardening class that graduated almost two years ago.

How on earth did six landscape gardeners from Lakeview wind up hours away, working on the streets of Mountainside in the middle of the night?

"You like them?" Hennessy asks, following my gaze.

I have no idea how to answer.

"What about those?" He points through the window and I follow his finger to where another group of six identical brown-clad women are washing the windows of a shop that clearly closed for the day hours earlier. "My father bought a batch just like that to replace his household staff, which is scheduled to expire next week. They should be here in a couple of days."

The lump in my throat threatens to choke me. *He's talking about the windows.* Please *let him be talking about the windows.*

But he isn't. Windows won't replace a household staff. Yet a crew of identical girls from Lakeview's year-eighteen manual labor division will do that nicely.

I can't answer. I am horrified beyond words.

I understand now why Lakeview has no residential or industrial ward.

Classes that graduate from my native city don't go to work for the glory of Lakeview after all.

My father bought a batch. . . .

I feel like I'm going to be sick.

I look at Trigger and find his jaw clenched. His hands grip the edges of his seat. He is fighting to control his tongue, or his fists, or whatever part of him most wants to express the rage we're both feeling as this new reality crashes over us.

It's time to go. It's time for us to leave the car and run off into the city to take what we need to survive in the wild.

It's time to leave both Lakeview and Mountainside in the dust.

I lay one hand on his shoulder. He turns to look at me. My mouth is open, ready to put our plan in motion.

Then the driver slows the car in front of a tall, ornate gate set just back from the road. "Welcome home, Ms. Whitmore."

What? *No.*

I can only stare in terrified silence as he presses a button at the gate and tells the face that appears on the screen that he has brought Waverly Whitmore home.

"Excuse me?" the black-clad soldier on-screen says. "Ms. Whitmore went to bed hours ago."

The driver chuckles. "You're mistaken." He angles the screen until the soldier on it is looking right at me. The soldier scowls, then presses a button offscreen. The gate rolls open.

Hennessy's car pulls forward on its own, driving us past a manicured tiered lawn climbing the side of the mountain until we roll to a stop in front of a huge house eerily reminiscent of the Administrator's mansion, but built into the earth itself at the back.

My heart thumps in my ears. I can't get out. *I don't belong here.*

The tall, narrow front door flies open and a woman steps barefoot onto the broad front porch, wrapping a long pink robe tight around her slim hips. "Waverly Whitmore!" she snaps, bending to frown at me through the window. "Get out of the car!"

Trigger gets out and opens Margo's door. He gives me a reassuring look as I climb over her, and as he helps me out he whispers, "Get ready to run."

I'm more than ready. But when I stand at the edge of the driveway and look up at the woman in the pink robe, every

253

thought in my head deserts me. I am looking at an older version of myself.

Waverly's mother has my brown eyes, fair skin, and pointed chin. But her nose is different.

"Who the hell is that?" she demands, frowning at Trigger.

Before I can figure out how to answer, the front door opens again. A girl with my face and Poppy's smile comes jogging down the steps. "Hennessy!" she cries, without even a glance at me, and I realize he's gotten out of the car at my back. "Look! They've got it loaded already! Have you seen it yet? It'll be on every billboard in the city by tomorrow night."

She holds up a tablet, but before I can see what's on it, her gaze finds me.

Her jaw drops and her arm falls slack. "Mom . . ." Her voice is hoarse with shock. "What the *hell* is going on?"

Waverly's mother stares back and forth between us, both hands clasped over her mouth.

And before I can decide what to do, my focus is drawn down to the tablet hanging by Waverly's right knee. On its screen, I am shocked to see my own face, made up with the paint and glitter Margo and her friends wore at Seren's party. Standing just behind me in the image is Hennessy, whose arms are wrapped around my waist.

The caption beneath our smiling faces reads, "Don't miss the wedding of the century—a Network Four exclusive! Lady Waverly Whitmore + Sir Hennessy Chapman Forever!"

ACKNOWLEDGMENTS

This book could not have been written if not for the presence of several very important people in my life. I am thankful, as always, to my husband, who puts up with me on both the good days and the bad, and to my daughter and my son, for on-demand opinions from my target audience, as well as for their willingness to eat pizza when deadlines loom.

Thanks to Rinda Elliott, who helped me brainstorm *Brave New Girl* on the way from Oklahoma City to Dallas. Your friendship and willing ear mean so much to me.

Thanks also to Jennifer Lynn Barnes, for endless suggestions and opinions over weekly working lunches. Sometimes our lunches are the sanest hours of my week.

Endless gratitude to Sophie Jordan, Aprilynne Pike, and Kimberly Derting, who helped me figure out what this book was missing. I miss writing with you all in person!

And thanks most of all to my editor, Wendy Loggia, and to my agent, Merrilee Heifetz, who got the whole thing rolling. Your support means the world to me!

Can't wait to find out what happens next?

Here's a sneak peek at the sequel,

STRANGE NEW WORLD.

ONE

WAVERLY

I flop on my bed and touch the center of the screen covering the far wall of my bedroom. Rows of E-scape messages pop up. On the left edge of each message is a photo of the person who posted. Some of the messages are photographs. Others are video clips, playing silently because I've disabled the sound. I don't want to hear about all the fun people are having without me.

Suddenly my bedroom door slides open with a whisper, and I wave my hand in a swiping motion, closing the message stream. The screen flashes white, then becomes transparent, showing the colorful stripes of the wall beneath.

"Knock, knock," my father says from the doorway, even though the door is already open. I've set it to let him in but to keep my mother out. Of course, she can override the settings, but the fact that I want to keep her out will be enough to make my point.

My dad doesn't say anything, but I know he saw my screen.

He knows I was stalking the E-scape. "What, no production crew today?" He glances around my room in mock disbelief as he steps inside carrying a covered tray.

"What would be the point?" I get up, and the white comforter smooths itself out, leaving a flawless, wrinkle-free finish, erasing any evidence that I was there. "You think the world wants to see me sitting here staring at the wall?"

He smiles as he sets the tray on my dresser. "The world wants to see everything you do. They didn't dub you and Hennessy digicast royalty for nothing."

I shrug. I have fun playing princess on camera. I don't even mind being recognized in public—that's really the only reason I go out. But my father knows me like my millions of followers never will.

"I hear we have attendants to do that." I nod at the tray.

"I am aware," my dad says with one brow raised. "But when your daughter already has everything—including the number-one ranked digicast worldwide—sometimes the only thing left to give her is the personal touch."

"That is *so* cheesy." I roll my eyes, but I can't hide my smile.

"Actually, it's chocolatey." He lifts the lid from the tray, revealing two steaming mugs of something divinely sweet-smelling. "Organic cocoa."

"*Mom's* cocoa?"

He nods. "First shipment of the season."

Okay, yes. It's just hot chocolate. Except that the cocoa beans this chocolate comes from are organic, grown overseas in actual dirt and watered by hand. Harvested by hand. Dried and processed by hand. Packaged by hand.

All that specialized labor makes the cocoa insanely expensive.

"And . . ." My father lifts a smaller dome lid from an opaque glass bowl at the back of the tray. "Hand-cut chocolate-hazelnut marshmallows."

"Does Mom know you dug into her stash?" I grab a mug and use a tiny set of tongs to drop two large, fluffy marshmallows into it. I glance at the reading on the side of the mug. It's set to keep the contents at the perfect drinking temperature.

"Let me worry about your mother." My dad picks up his own mug, then settles into my desk chair as I sink onto the edge of my bed. "So . . ." He takes sip of cocoa. "Why are you grounded this time?"

I tuck my legs beneath me and cradle my mug. "I honestly have no idea." My father scoffs, but I talk over his skepticism. "No, really. She said Seren's party would be nothing but trouble, and when I accused her of not trusting me, she grounded me from the party she already didn't want me to go to. It's like she set me up."

My father frowns. "That doesn't sound much like your mother."

"I know." Normally, my mother is logical to a fault, but . . . "It's like she has something against Seren. She grounded me last year on his birthday too." I pluck one of the soggy marshmallows from my cocoa and bite into it, frowning as I chew. "And she dragged us all on vacation during Sophia's birthday party this year, remember? Maybe it's not just Seren she doesn't like, but his whole family."

"I think you're reading a little too much into it," my dad says.

"Or maybe it's Seren and Sophia's mother. The Administrator could creep anyone out." I take the first sip from my mug. It's decadently sweet, yet creamy. The kind of thing I should be drinking on camera.

"The Administrator is just doing her job."

"No, she's *living* her job. You run all of Digicore, but you don't go around making people call you the CEO, do you?"

My father laughs, and chocolate sloshes near the edge of his mug. "So why is missing this party such a tragedy, anyway?" he asks. "How is it better than the one you went to last week or the one you'll go to next week?"

"I don't party *every* weekend," I insist. But I'm just avoiding the question. My father may know me better than my friends and followers do, but the me he knows is still his little girl—even if only for a few more weeks.

"I mean, it's not like you're really missing out on anything," he says. "There's still a video block at Lakeview, right?"

My silent sip tells him more than actually answering would.

"Ah. That's it," he says. "What happens in Lakeview stays in Lakeview, right? Because of the video blackout."

There are only two parties a year in Lakeview: Seren's birthday party and Sophia's birthday party. And because it's a digital dark zone—meaning no video—you can do whatever you want at a Lane party without worrying about it showing up on the E-scape. Or the public streams. For one night only, it's like you don't exist, except to the other people in the room.

"We can cancel the digicast, Waverly," my father says, his brow furrowed in concern. "I said from the beginning, as soon as it stops being fun—"

"No! I love the show." Even though it means the entire world sees everything that happens in my life—my mom actually got hate pings tonight for grounding me from Seren's party, which feels a little bit like a victory, considering that I'm stuck at home. "Besides, the bonding ceremony is next week. The ratings might actually outshine the proposal."

I smile just thinking about that episode. Hennessy put so

much work into keeping his proposal a secret from me, into truly surprising me for the first time since the first episode aired, and for a few minutes, in spite of the cameras, it felt like just the two of us, alone in the National Garden, surrounded by a thousand different kinds of roses. He had one in his hand as he dropped to one knee, and—

I blink, shaking off the memory, and find my father watching me, the ghost of a smile haunting the corners of his mouth.

"Speaking of which . . . ," I say, before he can get all emotional and remind me that we can still delay the whole thing by a couple of years. "I've finally decided for sure about my dress. I haven't even shown Mom yet!" With my mug in one hand, I swipe in the direction of my screen and the data-glass lights up, showing every app I left running when I turned it off. I gesture toward the one in the top right corner, and it zooms into the center of the wall, showing a two-foot-tall interactive image of my wedding dress.

"One hundred percent," I command as I stand and set my mug on my night table. Fabric rustles behind me as my comforter smooths itself out again, and I shrug out of my robe on my way toward the screen as the dress grows to its full size.

"Dressing room," I command, now wearing only a black virtu-fit body glove. I step in front of the glass, and the image on-screen turns the reflection of my bedroom into the inside of an old-fashioned dressing room, with the last few ensembles I bought hanging on hooks on the walls, waiting to be tried on. In the center of the screen, my dress rotates until I'm looking at the back of it. I hold my hands up and the dress rises, then falls over my reflection.

I'm wearing my wedding dress.

"Oh . . ." My father stands and steps forward until his image is in the dressing room with me. It's strange to see him there. I shop for clothes with my mom all the time, but rarely with my dad. But the look on his face is exactly what I was hoping for. "You look *beautiful*, sweetheart."

He hasn't seen anything yet.

"Hair," I command. "Final selection." The image on-screen blurs for an instant, then comes back into focus. My hair is now swept into a cluster of dark, glossy curls dusted with glitter. I turn, and my reflection turns on the screen, to show him the back of my updo.

"Makeup," I say as I face the mirror again. "Semifinal selection, 'Morning Dew.'"

My face blurs, then focuses with one of my favorite looks in place—a natural-but-better look, with rosy cheeks, nude lipstick, subtle contouring, and slightly dramatic eye makeup, to draw people's focus where I want it. To my best feature.

"Very elegant," my father says. I know that's one of only three or four phrases he has to describe any look I show him, but I also know he means it. I can see it in his eyes.

"Thanks." I swipe my hand across the screen and the app minimizes; then the screen flashes white and returns to its translucent sleep-state. "We've gotten a lot of pings asking for a glimpse of the dress, but I decided to keep it secret." I shrug into my robe again and reclaim my cocoa. "It'll play better on the digicast if everyone's anticipating the reveal."

"Well, I think anything you chose would have looked wonderful on you, but that is truly stunning, Waverly." He frowns. "I won't tell your mother I've seen it, but you should show her soon, before her feelings are hurt."

"I would have shown her tonight if she hadn't grounded me."

A beep echoes from my father's pocket, and I swallow a bitter lump of disappointment. "Work calls," he says, pulling his tablet out to glance at it

"I know. It always does. Thanks for the cocoa." I lift my mug in a gesture of appreciation as he heads for the door.

"I can't believe my baby's about to get married," he says as the door opens. "You know, we could put this off for a couple more years. Seventeen is so young."

"I'll be eighteen in a month," I remind him. I don't want to wait. I can't *afford* to wait. "You know what the doctor said."

"I know. And I understand. I just want you to be happy. Good night, sweetheart." But his happy, supportive expression slips for just a second before the door slides closed.

Alone again, I swipe at the screen to wake up the glass. "Send someone to remove this tray," I command.

"Command received," a sexy male voice responds. "An attendant will come for it immediately."

Normally, my E-scape would be filled with video clips and messages, showing my friends dancing, eating, and generally looking gorgeous and glamorous without me, but thanks to the video ban from Lakeview, all I get are the messages they've spoken into their tablets.

Before I open the messages, I disable the activity notification so no one will know I'm reading streams from a party I'm not at. As far as they're all concerned, I'm much too busy with wedding preparations to bother.

I open the first message.

SURPRISE OF THE NIGHT! WAVERLY WHITMORE SHOWS UP! RUMOR HAS IT SHE'S WEARING A *BORROWED* DRESS, BUT SHE *OWNED* THE LOOK TONIGHT!

Wait, what?

Frowning, I opening message after message, as fast as I can read them. They detail the party menu and the guest list. They talk about some scandalous invasion of the event by Lakeview soldiers searching for a fugitive—*what???*—and there's an entire thread dedicated to couples who turned the dance floor into a private make-out session.

But then there it is again. Another reference to me at the party.

It's a joke. It has to be. My friends are pranking me because I missed the best party of the year. But it's not funny.

Irritated, I close the messages and check my private pings instead. While I'm reading, the attendant comes in and removes the tray and used dishes. I don't recognize the name embroidered on her uniform, but I know her face. It's the same as all our other attendants, from a batch that matured two years ago.

When she leaves, I glance at the top left corner of the glass for the time. Twelve-twenty. The party ended nearly half an hour ago.

A new ping appears from the network that airs my digistream. I open it, and an image takes over half of the glass. It's the new ad for the season finale—the wedding episode. It shows Hennessy and me, looking hot as hell, his arms wrapped around me, this smoldering look in his eyes that millions of girls all over the world wish he would turn on them.

But he's all mine.

The ad flashes, *Don't miss the wedding of the century—a Network Four exclusive! Lady Waverly Whitmore + Sir Hennessy Chapman Forever!*

I squeal in delight and swipe the screen off. Then I strip out of my robe and leotard and throw on some clothes. I grab my mini-glass tablet on the way out of my room, tapping through the menus as I head down the hall toward my mother's room to show her.

She's not in her room. She's not in her office either. But then I hear her voice and feel a draft from downstairs. The front door is standing wide open.

"Waverly Whitmore!" my mother snaps. "Get out of the car!"

Huh?

I jog down the stairs, clutching my tablet in my left hand, but I forget all about my mother when I look beyond her to see Hennessy getting out of a long black car. "Look! They've got it loaded already!" I hold up the tablet to show him the image. "Have you seen it yet? It'll be on every billboard in the city by tomorrow night."

But then my focus settles on the girl standing next to him, and my hand falls limp at my side. My jaw literally drops. "What the *hell* is going on?"

The girl standing next to my fiancé? She's wearing my face.

Excerpt copyright © 2017 by Rachel Vincent.
Published by Delacorte Press,
an imprint of Random House Children's Books,
a division of Penguin Random House LLC, New York.

From *New York Times* bestselling auth

RACHEL VINCENT

The start of a pulse-pounding duology!

 KATHERINE TEGEN BOOKS
An Imprint of HarperCollins Publishers

www.epicreads.c